LOVELORN

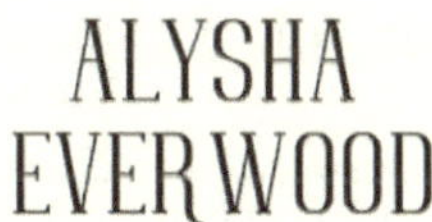

Lovelorn: Book 1 of The Misfortunates

Cover Design: Alysha Everwood

Editor: Lauren Baker, Tea and Tales LLC

ISBN(paperback): 979-8-9995064-2-9

ISBN(E-book): 979-8-9995064-3-6

-Eros

To the ones who have always watched from the sidelines as love passed you by, and the ones who thought something was wrong with them; you are not broken.

Prologue

Love. Everyone desires it, but not all find it. Sometimes it is something chosen, and other times it's an out-of-control fire, burning hot through one's veins, eating through all logic and rationality. They say love can hurt, but what they don't tell you is what can twist your heart even more, is never being loved. It has never chosen me despite me putting my heart out there just to be scorned.

Desire and lust are one thing, and that can be received and given without love ever being present. But I want the yearning, the pining, the feather light brush of knuckles against the soft flesh of my cheek, the tangle of fingers before a kiss brushes over skin, the talks that fade into the night under a moonlit sky. I want to be known, to be seen, to be accepted for all I am and all that I am not.

But some ancestor of mine decided to muck things up with Aphrodite, and yes, I mean *the* goddess, so now I'm stuck to suffer a curse of unrequited love. But does that keep me from attempting to find someone who can love me? No, but it does make me an idiot who thinks true love can break a centuries long curse.

1

ALORA

I promised myself I wouldn't cry this time. But inevitably, the tears welled up, pouring from my eyes like summer rain, hot and sticky on my cheeks, which were already red from rejection.

"You're wonderful, truly. You have a lovely personality; you're funny, smart, kind, and not horrible to look at." Gregory looked at me with a patronizing gaze, and my brows furrowed at the compliment, or insult rather. I know I'm not the most confident woman, but my looks aren't atrocious. "But I'm afraid there's a lack of feeling

on my part."

After the first few rejections, I've learned to keep my tears at bay until we fully part ways, so I nod like I always do and say my understanding of his choice.

"Really, I didn't want to hurt you." He says it with so much pity that it feels patronizing.

"I understand. It's alright." It wasn't, but that's not his fault.

"See, you're so great, you're being so great about this. I was worried you'd freak out given the timing." He chuckles breathily, and my brows quirk up at this.

"What do you mean?"

"Well, you know...since you have denied all of my advances for a physical relationship, I didn't want you to think that's why I'm breaking things off."

"Is that why you're breaking things off?" He looks anywhere but at my eyes now, scratching the back of his head, and I sigh internally.

"You could have said something at the beginni—"

"I would've..." he interrupts. "But I thought if I charmed you enough and pretended to care about your hobbies that—" He trails off, seeming to regret his word

choices. Anger was boiling in my belly now, but I never let it bubble over the surface. Instead, I asked calmly.

"That you ***what****?"*

Silence. Oh, now he wants to be silent.

"That if you pretended to be the perfect guy for me, you'd inevitably bed me?" How do I always fall for men like this? All wrapped up in a nice bow, presenting me with the perfect idea of a man, just to want nothing more than my body.

His cheeks flushed as he scratched his brow.

"We had fun, did we not? I was simply hoping to get more out of this. I mean, you're not the kind of girl a man weds." My breath gets caught in my throat at this, my lips thinning as I look away.

"I—I shouldn't have said that. I apologize." He bends down to match my height, nervously attempting to catch my gaze.

"As I said before, I understand and agree it is best we part ways." I don't leave room for him to say more, turning briskly to return to my cottage.

I shouldn't be crying over him; I hadn't even reached the point of loving him, but I was so swept up by his charm that I missed the signs of uninterest that seem so clear in hindsight. *"Not the kind of girl a man weds."* What does that mean? I know I shied away from his attempts at touch, even if they were innocent, but I hadn't fallen in love with him yet and thus had no desire but to get to know him intellectually.

Perhaps I'm broken. Maybe it's a result of this stupid curse. Would physical intimacy lead a man to fall in love with me? If that is the only way to break this curse, I fear I will never break it, for that is not something I'm even sure I'm willing to give unless love was sitting on both sides of the table.

It wasn't until I reached teen hood that I truly felt the weight of the curse. While everyone else was falling for whoever they fancied, I was left on the sidelines, watching as people experienced something I never would.

No one talks about the mental and emotional turmoil that comes from never experiencing young love, from never feeling truly desirable. You question if love is even something you're worthy of. Of course, I had the love of my mother and friends, but it is not a replacement for romantic love. I swear, if one more person tells me to just love myself or that it will come when I least expect it, I'm going to throw them in a ditch.

Now, with Mother gone, and all my friends having found husbands and moved on with their lives, loneliness feels like an ever-present, suffocating phantom. I know it's the curse, but with rejection after rejection, it's hard not to believe there's something wrong with me.

Looking at myself in the mirror, I take in my appearance. My long dark waves are a bit frizzy from the misty mornings of early spring, my brown eyes a little red and puffy from crying, my pale olive skin peeking through the makeup where my tears created a trail. My gaze lingers on the curve of my hips, wider than I'd like them to be, and my stomach, which has a soft edge to it.

"I am beautiful." I tell my reflection, but no matter how many times I repeat the words, my brain never seems to fully believe them. Breathing deeply, I wipe the remnants of tears away and paste on a smile. Per-

haps a nice afternoon walk in the woods would cheer me up.

Living in the cottage on the grounds of a vineyard, you'd think me well off, but I was simply granted a home here by my mother's best friend and her husband, a doctor. I often cook their meals as payment, and they're kind enough to allow me to dine with them. But that often results in an attempt to find me a suitor, which has undoubtedly given me more tears than anything else. That's why my nature walks have become a must, and luckily, my cottage nears the edge of the forest; my place of solace.

Hating how the twigs and rocks dig into the bottom of my feet through my slippers, I opt for my mother's old gardening boots she left me, the leather worn and a bit scuffed, but that's what makes them all the more special.

Traipsing through the trees, I love the way my dress ripples in the wind, the smell of nature inviting me in like a warm hug, mending the smallest of cracks in my soul, if only for a moment. The familiar sounds of forest animals stepping out from hiding warm my heart as the cold, wet nose of a fawn brushes against my fingertips.

"Hello, beautiful." I stroke her snout as she closes her eyes in contentment. A few squirrels perch up on a branch, chittering excitedly, a fox scurrying around my legs, its bushy tail swinging back and forth as a few rabbits circle my feet.

"I know what you all want." Digging into my pocket that I sewed in just for this occasion, I pulled out a few chunks of day-old bread and a some dried berries. Sprinkling the crumbs around the forest floor, I watch with a wide grin as they nibble away. The rhythmic flapping of wings and birdsong draws me further into the trees, farther than I've been before, where a hazy glow of sunlight filters through the branches, landing upon marbled ruins in majestic beams.

I gasp at its beauty, pale pink flowers and ivy intertwining between the cracks, vibrant moss blanketing the ground and draping over broken pillars like fabric. A set of steps at the center breaks off as if ascending to another realm, framed by an arch that is mostly intact save for a few chips and cracks. A pair of doves flap gently down to me before flying to perch on the arch as if beckoning me forward. Curious, my feet leave the rough terrain of the forest, stepping upon the soft mossy ground and up the marbled steps.

This must be where humans used to commune with the gods. Most don't much believe anymore, but given my curse, I'd say that's pretty good evidence of their existence. Once again, thanks a lot, great, great, *not so great*, great, grandfather. How have I never stumbled upon this place before?

Looking farther ahead, I notice half a wall containing a painting, swirling with beautiful, smooth brushstrokes depicting the gods. All those years of mother searching for answers, the many years since her death that I've been scouring book after book for something–*anything*, only to end up empty handed. But now–by fate or by chance–I stand amidst the ancient ruins of the very ones who could help me. My eyes land on Aphrodite, where she stands inside a large seashell, her hair wrapped around the frame of her body.

"That's it! I can call upon Aphrodite and see if she

can break my curse. Who better to understand my plight than the goddess of love?" I'm not the one she technically cursed, so maybe she'll grant me some leniency. My heart skitters in my chest, hope turning the corners of my lips for the first time since I discovered my curse.

"Okay, okay! Focus." I say aloud to myself, taking a deep breath.

I've read many books in my time, considering I can't find my own love in the real world, I find it in stories, so romance novels are my forte. However, I have gained a particular interest in the gods as I worked to undo the curse, but I've never been able to find a ruin before. They're said to be a direct link to Olympus. Perhaps I've caught a break for a change. Oh no, maybe I shouldn't have said that. Should I knock on wood? Erm—I should knock on wood. Quickly running to the nearest tree, I lightly rap my knuckles on the trunk, hoping I didn't jinx myself.

"Alright— "I step up to the edge of where the stairs end. Remembering a way to make a summons from one of the books I found on Greek deities, I take the pin from my hair and use the sharp point to prick my finger. Letting the blood pool at the tip, a crimson drop falls onto the mossy ground below as I speak my request:

Aphrodite, I call on thee,
Hear my plea, hear my plea.
Goddess of love, I need thine heed.
Your guidance for my heart's deepest need.

I pull my finger back after the moss drinks up the fifth drop of blood, waiting in anticipation.

Eight, nine, ten seconds pass...nothing.

Was my phrasing poor? I figured a rhyme couldn't hurt. Disappointment nearly takes root before my eyes land once again upon the painting where a chubby cherub floats in a cloud with their bow drawn, an arrow ready to fly.

"CUPID!" If Aphrodite can't help, maybe he can. Placing my finger back over the land, the blood beads up once again. Now to call upon the god.

Cupid with a striking arrow,
Help me now to free my sparrow.
Guidance that I ask of thee,
I call on your divinity.

As the last drop falls, flowers begin to sprout from the ground, petal after petal stacking on top of each other as ivy tangles in between to form a figure, until a polished marble statue of a man with wings stands solid in the moss. I stare at the stone for a moment, the sun glittering on its surface. Inching my head forward, I wait for something to happen.

Then, a warm puff of air tickles my neck as a melodious voice whispers in my ear.

"You called?"

My heart nearly leaps from my chest as I whirl around, losing my footing and almost plummeting into the statue, but slender fingers gently wrap around my wrist, pulling me back from the edge.

"Already wanting to fall into my arms, hmm? And that's just my statue. It does me quite the justice, does it not?" The man poses like the marble figure, my shocked eyes falling between the two—an uncanny match. But unlike the stone, he has no wings. His hair sits in beautiful curls atop his head, a light blonde color I've never seen before, with a faint rosy hue to it.

I open my mouth to speak, but nothing comes out.

"Ahh, speechless in my presence. That's quite alright. Take your time." He says, sending me a wink.

I can't help but follow his movements with my eyes as he circles around me. A red sash wrapped diagonally down his chest, meeting the fabric at his waist, leaves his tall frame—lean and chiseled with muscle—exposed.

"I quite enjoyed your plea. Very rhymey. Yes, I know that's not a word, but I'm a god, so now it is." He flashes me a bright smile.

"Y—you're Cupid? But where—where are your wings?"

"Ahh, right!" he stops in front of me, stretching the muscles of his back, two feathered wings flapping out in an astounding span.

"And the name's actually Eros, god of love, desire,

and passion." His wings draw in to rest closer to his body.

"Aren't you supposed to be a chubby cherub wearing a diaper?" I ask.

"That was one time! I get a bit too drunk, lose a bet, and eat a little too much at one of Dionysus's parties, and I never live it down. They just had to put it down in pigments." He throws his hands out in exasperation, and I quirk a brow at him before schooling my features, not sure if I'm allowed to questioningly look at a god. "As you can see, my physique is not like that painting." He gestures down his body with a cheeky smirk.

"I—I do see." I say through a breathy laugh, quickly everting my eyes when he catches me staring.

"Anywho!" he waves a hand through the air, and I can't help but furrow my brows at a god's use of the word. "What can the god of love do for you?" He asks, pointing a finger at me with a charming smile.

"Well, I'm cursed."

"Cursed? Whatever could a lovely lady like yourself have done to get cursed?"

"It was actually an ancestor of mine; he upset Aphrodite." I can't help the slight edge of bitterness that falls from my tongue.

"Ahh, Mother. Her curses are a thing of beauty, but it's quite unfortunate you must suffer from it as well. What is the consequence of this curse?"

"I'm to suffer from unrequited love. I'm free to love, but no one will ever love me back." I say softly, unable to hide the sorrow from my voice.

"I see." His face softens, an edge of sadness lingering in his tone as if he understands. But just as quickly, his face perks up as he walks closer.

"I will help you!" He nods.

"You will?" I light up at this, wondering if I truly have a chance to find love.

"But of course. We don't get as many prayers as we once did, and the ones who usually call upon me are stubble-faced men, so you're quite the welcomed change." He winks, a little gleam in his pale blue eyes as he circles me with his slow steps, once again.

"We will try everything under Helios to get someone to fall in love with you. Perhaps we could start off with a makeover. Not that you aren't a beauty of your own, but I can make you truly a sight to behold to all mankind."

"Erm—thank you?" My voice rises in question, not sure if that was a jab at my current state.

"Oh, it is my pleasure, this is one of my favorite parts. Maybe we should begin with your shoes. What is this monstrosity?" He gestures from my worn boots to my dress with a slight grimace.

"It's called practicality. Slippers don't make for great footwear in the forest." His eyes widen, and I immediately attempt to fix my mistake. Perhaps that was not the best way to address a god.

"I'm sorry, I mean—it's not erm..."

"Fret not, my love. I'm not opposed to reverence, but with many decades of blubbering buffoons who are too lazy to try and understand a woman, I quite like the normalcy in which you address me." He gives me that signature smirk of his again, and if he weren't the god of love, I'd be blushing, but flirting is in his repertoire.

"Now, to get started." He claps his hands together.

"Would you rather fly or teleport?"

2

EROS

Before her question can worry her brow, I snap my fingers, our bodies teleporting to my place on Mount Olympus.

"What just—?" She holds her arms out beside her to steady herself, looking around in bewilderment. "I—erm—could you please not do that again without warn—" Her hands fly over her stomach, cheeks puffing out before she runs to one of my houseplants to retch.

"Oh, dear one." I hesitantly pat her back with a

grimace as she empties her guts all over poor Radford, my beautifully loyal fern. "You have my word; I will warn you in advance."

"Thank you!" She bashfully wipes her mouth with the back of her hand.

"May I offer you a complimentary mint?" I hold out my hand, a silver dish with the lovely nymph's homemade sugared herbal leaves.

She gratefully takes the treat and places it on her tongue, sighing in relief at the calm it brings to her stomach, as well as ridding her breath of the acidic tinge the sickness left in her mouth.

"I do apologize for the brisk transportation, but I realized once the words left my lips that you did not seem like a flying kind of person."

"I don't think I care for either." She chuckles softly as she sucks on the mint.

"Welcome to my lovely abode." I gesture to the grandeur around her, watching as she takes in the Ionic pillars dressed in my thorny roses.

"These are beautiful." Her dainty fingers brush over the petals of a blush pink rose.

"Mmm, yes," my fingers coil around the stem of one. "A reminder that though flourishing love can be beautiful–" I pluck the rose from its thorny body. "It can also prick you and suck out all hope from your veins, draining the blood from your beating heart." I crush the petals in my fist as I glare at the delicate botany before quickly replacing it with a bright smile that makes Alora's brows shoot up, but there's a softness of sympathy resting in her eyes that has not been shown to me before.

"Ahem." I clear my throat, trying to smooth over my teensy outburst. "Take a gander outside." I gesture towards the beautiful open arches that allow a stunning view of the swirling clouds of Olympus, a gentle breeze wafting over us. The slick stone floors glitter with gold in the sunlight as Alora's careful steps lead her to the stunning view.

"Oh my!" She inches closer, giggling as her fingers reach through the white vapor, my heart warming at the sound not so often heard these days.

"Is this real? Or have I sustained a head injury?" She asks in wonder, making me chuckle.

"I assure you, this is all very real, but I know I'm quite the dream." I puff out my chest, my chiseled form catching the rays of sun just right. She turns enough to arch those lovely dark brows at me with a light scoff.

"Now, shall we begin with—"

"Oh, hello little guy!" Alora crouches down where Muggsy, my trusty hare, hops at her feet.

"Ahh, of course. How could I forget to allow Muggsy his introduction?" Her fingers gently brush his fur, and he nuzzles further into her hand.

"My lovely companion, your cuteness is revered, but it is interfering with my work." If a hare could glare, that's what his small dark eyes send me before hopping into Alora's arms and snuggling up to her.

"Traitor." I whisper at him with narrowed eyes. The twitch of his ears tells me he heard me, but the little pest ignores me.

"Alright, well, since he insists on outdoing my splendor with his adorableness, why don't we take a look at greatest hits—or misses, my apologies." I walk over to the birdbath in the garden, Alora's small steps following curiously after.

"Wait, you're going to make me watch my most embarrassing moments in regard to love?"

"Oh, don't worry. I won't pry into any intimate moments, but what better way to help you than to see where things have gone wrong?"

I have no intimate moments. She whispers under her breath, imperceptible to the human ear, but I'm a god. My heart hurts for her, and I know she must be feeling vulnerable right now, so I pretend I didn't hear.

"Okay–Muggsy, I'm going to need your moral support for this." She scratches the hare behind his ear.

Waving my hand over the surface of the water, it ripples before taking form as a memory.

"I'm sorry, it just isn't going to work between us." A man with copious amounts of gel slicking his hair back says, without even a hint of actual apology in his tone.

"You're wonderful, but I just don't see a future with you."

"I don't feel the same; I love someone else."

"For heaven's sake, you won't even let me make it

to your brassiere." Him, I'd like to shoot with just a regular arrow for that ridiculous remark.

"You're sweet, but I only see you as a friend. It will never be more." I take a chance and glance at Alora, who hugs Muggsy to her chest, her face a mix of embarrassment and pain, and a pang of guilt hits me deep in my chest.

Lastly, we watch her most recent rejection that led her to call upon me. I wave the image away when a tear silently makes its way down her cheek.

"I'm sorry you've had to endure that."

She nods politely as Muggsy nuzzles farther into her arms.

"When I'm done, you are going to be the most desirable woman, second to Aphrodite, of course. Let's stay on Mother's good side." I chuckle and hope she doesn't see the glint of fear in my eyes. Mother is very nurturing, but she is not to be crossed, as Alora well knows.

"Now, if you'll follow me to where the magic happens." I wave her forward as I lead us back inside.

"Ah, I just heard that out loud." I quickly catch myself, realizing how that could come off sexually. "Not *that* kind of magic." I assure her, and she chuckles, following me with quiet steps.

Bringing her to a dais surrounded by a horseshoe of ornate brass mirrors, I snap my fingers, a changing room with drapes appearing off to the side.

"Alright!" I clap my hands together excitedly. "This is my favorite part."

"Is there some sort of magic in the attire? Why not just shoot an arrow?"

"Given your situation being more... complex, it wouldn't hurt to add a little extra flair before we go in search of a perfect match."

"Alright." She says, her tone betraying her lack of confidence in the plan. Begrudgingly, she places Muggsy down on the pleated velvet stool while I lounge in the chair beside it, intertwining my fingers behind my head.

"And cue the montage." Once again, she quirks that brow at me, and I smile brightly until I see a crack of one at her lips. Shaking her head, she steps behind the drapes, and with a snap of my fingers, I laugh at her shocked gasp as a full set of clothes appears on her body, accompanied by hair and makeup.

"I look ridiculous; what is this?" She steps out with a very cute scowl on her face as she messes with the layers upon layers of frills and lace, her makeup pale and bright, her hair a nest of curls high upon her head.

"Not everyone can pull off a full Marie. You know I was the one who gave her that signature style."

"Why am I not surprised?" The barest of smiles graces her lips, and I smile back, glad to help ease her mind away from the heartache.

"I say you own it, and you'll certainly catch some eyes."

"Absolutely not. Next." She walks back inside, and I find myself comforted by the easy flow of our interaction. My fingers snap *three, four, five* times, and I couldn't help but put her in some obviously poor choices.

A dress that looks like a wedding cake, aglow with candles, wax dripping down the dress.

"I'm going to combust." she says, holding her arms

out at her sides to avoid the flames.

A dress made of material so shiny, I can barely even look at her with its blinding reflection.

"I look like a chandelier."

A pastel version of a sea pirate, complete with an embroidered eye patch and a live parrot. This one was particularly fun, causing me to hunch over in laughter as the bird poops on her shoulder.

"Are you even trying to help?" Her gaze is stern, but I can tell she's not truly upset.

"When was the last time you thought about your heartbreak?" She bites her bottom lip, looking down with a soft chuckle.

"Touché. I suppose you do know what you're doing after all." She turns on her heel, stepping back through the drapes.

"I'd say thanks, but I'm not sure if I should be flattered by your lack of confidence in me." I can't see her, but I know she rolled her eyes.

"Okay, last one." Snapping my fingers once more, I wait for her to step out, but she hesitates.

"Everything alright in there?" I stand from my

cushiony chair in concern.

"Yes, everything is fine. I just—" She doesn't finish as she steps out sheepishly, her cheeks red as she glances towards the floor. Muggsy chitters from his spot as I take in her appearance, astounding even myself with my work. The dusty blue fabric of the empire waist dress flows beautifully down her form, the skirts inlaid with floral details and accents of gold along the waist, neckline, and sleeves.

"I never truly feel beautiful, but this makes me feel so." Her brown eyes flick up to mine, and the soft fluttering of my wings makes me adjust at their involuntary movement.

"Alora, love," I step closer, brushing a soft wave from her face, my fingers grazing her hot cheek. "It is not just the appearance that decides beauty, but also heart and soul. You have both, and I'm sorry that any man has ever made you feel as if you don't." Her gaze searches mine, willing my words to be true, but I can tell that she doesn't quite believe it. Inhaling a sharp breath, I remove my hand and clear my throat as I step apart from her.

"Anywho, shall we go find you your match?"

3

ALORA

This time, he graciously warns me before teleporting us to a balcony overlooking a large garden party full of elaborately dressed people.

"Why are we here?"

"First, I have to know the extent of this curse, so pick your lucky lad, and I shall shoot him with my golden arrow. If he scales this ivy-dressed balcony to get to you, then perhaps we can find you a true love and bypass the curse with my arrows." He lets out an exaggerated exhale before leaning on the banister.

"My, that was a mouthful."

"And if he does obsessively fall in love with me, then what? That is not how I'd like to find love."

"You are most different from the burly men who've sought my counsel." He narrows his eyes at me. "I would just shoot them with a silver arrow to counteract the desire. However, depending upon the person, they could grow to hate you... deeply."

"Lovely." I say sarcastically. "Why silver?"

"Well, I used to use leaden arrows before silver, but those were slowly poisoning people and inadvertently killing them." He says nonchalantly as he overlooks the crowd of people, ignoring my horrified gaze.

"Oooh, how about that one?" I follow the point of his slender finger to a man with sandy blonde hair and a mustache. He's aesthetically pleasing, but as we continue watching him, he takes two flutes of champagne and downs them simultaneously before grabbing the rear of the poor servant girl, who yelps in surprise, skittering away in haste.

"Hmm, never mind that one." Eros grimaces beside me, and I'm grateful I don't have to say my disdain aloud.

"He looks nice." I point to a dark-haired man by the fountain, smelling the flowers nearby.

"Alrighty. One dark-haired male coming right up." In a poof of gold haze, a bow appears in his hand, a quiver of arrows on his back. Drawing back one of the gold-tipped arrows, I watch as it flies through the air, hitting the man right at the heart before disappearing a moment later. I wait with bated breath for something to happen, but the man remains entranced by the flowers.

"Huh—" Eros holds up one of his arrows, inspecting it with a quirked brow. "I don't usually have performance issues." He shrugs casually, and I can't help the chuckle that falls from me, his gaze partially flicking to mine with a small curl of his lips. But once my laughter fades, that last bit of hope I was clinging onto shrivels into ash; our little experiment was a failure. "Worry not, my dear one. That was just the first step. I have more in store."

"Now, how's your flirting game?"

4

EROS

"My flirting game?" She furrows those brows at me again.

"Yes, you know—how you woo a suitor. Do you bat your eyelashes? Do you gently touch their arm as they talk? Do you fake laugh at their jokes?"

"Why would I fake laugh at their jokes?"

"To pretend that they're funny, so they know you're interested in courting."

"I don't want to feign interest. What if I pretend to find a very stale man's jokes funny, then he does fall in love with me, and I'm stuck listening to horrible jokes."

"Hmm. So, you don't just want a companion?"

She sighs heavily at my question.

"I want companionship, but I don't just want someone for the sake of not being alone. Some people would say I'm too picky or my standards are too high, but why do we settle for less than what we want and what we deserve?" Her words strike a chord with me, and I realize how many people I've assisted who settle for the first person they swoon over, inevitably ending in disaster. Of course, sometimes the first love works out, but it's very rare.

"Alora Meadows, you are quite odd. And I mean that as a compliment." I rush to add the last bit when she narrows her eyes at me.

"I find you intriguing."

"Intriguing how?"

"Well, as an immortal being, I've had my fair share of relationships, but only one that was true love." I don't know why I opened this door that I've tried so hard to keep shut to block out the pain. "It may come as a surprise, but I don't much believe in love anymore." I state simply.

"What? But how can you not believe in love when that is the very thing you create?"

"I don't so much as create it, but rather provide the possibility of it being there to begin with."

"Sure, my arrows can cause infatuation, but that is not love; it's more an obsession with the idea of it. However, the potential for love being found is what I provide."

"And you found it?"

"Once." I look off into the distance before quickly collecting myself. "But let's not focus on me. This is about you, and me helping to open the doors for you to receive love."

"Now, perhaps it's best to have a demonstration. Select a man of your choosing, and let's see what you've got."

"Erm—alright." She hesitantly walks up to a man with dirty blonde hair and a neatly trimmed beard to match. His eyes meet hers as her small stature stands before him with a gentle smile.

Good start.

"A fine day out today." She glances around, gesturing at the flowers in bloom.

Oh, my love. Not weather talk.

"It is indeed."

"I erm... I love your cummerbund." He looks at her quizzically before hesitantly thanking her. **(My gods are you seeing this atrocious attempt? Yes, you. The one reading these words with your dazzling eyes. I'd almost avert mine if it weren't so amusing.)**

"Is it silk?" Her voice softens on the last word, not quite confident in her question.

I mean, fabrics—we're talking fabrics when I said flirting. That's alright, that's alright. This is practice, I suppose.

"Satin." His tone is dull and slightly annoyed.

What a rude man. I mean yes, it's not great conversation, but he could at least be a gentleman, for my-self's sake.

"Right, well, it's a lovely color." He gives a disinterested smile.

"If you'll excuse me, I think someone has called for me."

Her shoulders sink as she watches him retreat.

"That was you flirting?" She startles when I pop up beside her, a hand flying to rest over her heart.

"Gods, could you not just appear like that?" Her eyes go wide as her brows furrow in apology.

"Oh, I mean, is that okay to say?" I chuckle at her constant worry that she'll offend me, as if she could.

"I love it when you use that kind of talk with me." I wink, sending her a wry smirk, to which she rolls her eyes.

"Wait! Are you wearing a suit? And your hair is different." She looks me up and down. I roll my shoulders back, my skin itching uncomfortably inside the fabric.

"Yes, but I much prefer my less modest attire, but I would stand out like a sore thumb in that."

"So, the flirting." She rocks back and forth on her heels.

"Well, that wasn't great, but you tried... kind of." I mean, cummerbunds, really?" I glance down at her as she shrugs, embarrassed.

"You put me on the spot; I couldn't think."

"You don't know how to flirt, do you?"

"I—uh—whaaat?" Her voice rises in pitch as she huffs a laugh.

"Oh dear." I pinch the bridge of my nose. "It's time for a lesson. Take notes."

Walking up to a blonde woman inspecting a rose bush, I glance back at Alora, making sure she's paying attention.

"I've always admired roses. They hold such beauty." Her blue eyes glance at me, taking me in from head to toe, a smile rising to her pink lips.

"Yes, they do." She twirls a piece of hair around her finger.

"Much like a beautiful woman." I lean down, gently plucking one from the stem, my eyes never leaving hers as I do so. "But I've always much preferred pink roses." I cover the petals with my hand before extending out a now pink-tinted rose, the same color as her dress. "To match the beautiful lady."

She gasps, placing a gloved hand over her mouth.

"Are you a magician?" She delicately takes the rose, placing it under her nose to take in the scent.

"You could say that."

"That was spectacular. Perhaps you could show me another magic trick sometime...in my garden?" She grins suggestively at me. Taking her hand in mine, I place a kiss over her fingers, looking at her through my lashes.

"Perhaps." She giggles, twirling yet another strand of hair.

When I turn around to Alora, a dumbfounded look crosses her face.

"Well?" I ask as I saunter back to her.

"You have an unfair advantage. I can't just magic my way into wooing a man."

"That was only part of it. Here, let's try. Okay, now give me your most flirty look."

Her lips stretch into a close-lipped smile, her eyes widening slightly.

"You're just smiling at me; show me desire."

"I don't think I can manufacture that and would feel quite silly trying."

"If you're going to look silly, this is the safe place to do it. Let's see it."

She tilts her head down, looking up at me through a narrowed gaze as she moves her eyebrows up, then down, not quite sure of herself.

"You look as though you're about to sneeze."

She scoffs, sending a frown my way that is actually quite cute.

"Okay, let's role-play a bit, shall we? I'll show you how it's done."

"Mmm... alright." Her voice is unsure as her eyes dart around nervously.

"This is quite the spectacle, is it not?" I look out over the garden with its lush greenery.

"It's very beautiful." She smiles softly.

"But not quite as beautiful as you." My gaze falls to her, and when she looks at me, I can see the flecks of gold

that the sunlight brings out in her eyes.

"Thank you!" She smiles, but her tone tells me that she thinks my compliment is simply part of the act, not truly believing herself to be beautiful. Stepping closer, I can practically feel her nerves going haywire in the space

between us.

"I don't come to these things often, but running into a lovely woman, such as yourself, has made the trip

worthwhile."

"I don't often run into men who look as if they're sculpted of marble."

My brows raise at her brazen compliment of my physique, not able to help the wide smile that forms on my lips.

"That is quite the compliment, coming from someone who looks like an ancient goddess, revered and worshipped." Her smile falters as a blush fans across her cheeks at this, and I take it a step further, inching down to whisper in her ear. "And I'd forever pray on my knees for you." I pull back slowly, stopping until our faces are close enough for our breaths to mingle, looking directly into those eyes.

She clears her throat, taking a step back.□

“Do you really... erm... flirt like that?” She fiddles with her necklace as her blush fades.

“I am the god of love after all. Mustn’t disappoint.” I say nonchalantly, but I don’t usually have this much fun flirting. “And you really do look beautiful, Alora.” She looks down, brushing a strand of hair behind her ear bashfully. This curse has really damaged the perception she has of herself, and now I wish I could go back in time and smite the ancestor responsible.

“Now, with what you’ve learned in mind, give it another go. Take your pick.” I gesture towards the selection of men around.

She shifts on her feet as she scans the garden, taking them all in. A hint of a smile rises at the corner of her lips when she lands on a man sitting on a bench by the hedges reading a book. Of course she’d choose someone who’s reading for leisure.

“I should’ve guessed a man like him would suit your fancy.” I tease.

“Well, I’m not sure if I’d fancy him. I don’t know him, but I wouldn’t be opposed to trying.”

“Now’s your chance.” She walks nervously towards

the handsome man, his hair sculpted perfectly atop his head, his chiseled features softening when Alora approaches. I'll admit, he's a stud, but he's got nothing on me.

"Hello, do you mind if I sit?" She smiles sheepishly at him, her hands clasped in front of her, fingers subtly fidgeting.

Aww, she's nervous. How cute.

"Be my guest." He scoots over, sending her a charming smile. Sitting beside him with her hands in her lap, I can see the wheels turning in her mind of what to do next.

"I don't see many people who appreciate the art of Josephina Mirez." She nods towards the book in his hands, a copy of "A Nature Incandescent."

"Hers are some of my favorite works." He smiles, leaning over to whisper to her.

"This is actually a first edition." Alora's eyes light up, and she turns to him so quickly, their noses almost brush. He chuckles as she looks at him with wide eyes.

"You're joking. Is it really?"

"See for yourself." He hands her the brown

leather-bound book, the pages rough at the edges. Alora holds it reverently, gently turning the pages, her fingers lightly skimming over the words.

"This is magnificent. However did you get your hands on a first edition?"

"Don't be jealous, but from the author herself." Her mouth drops open in shock before she quickly snaps it shut.

"My apologies, I was surprised, is all." Her cheeks flush with embarrassment.

"I find it charming." His brown eyes meet hers, her cheeks reddening at his comment.

"Oh, how incredibly rude I've been. I must be the one to apologize, as I have yet to ask your name."

"Alora, and may I ask yours?"

"Peter, Peter Wylington."

"Oh my, this is your estate?" Alora suddenly grows stiffer, her self-consciousness settling back in.

"It is indeed."

"Well, it's quite beautiful."

"Thank you, I take pride in my botanical skills."

"You've done this all yourself?" She looks at him

once again in surprise, and he chuckles.

She really is quite expressive.

"With some help from my sisters. They'd kill me if I took all the credit."

"I just find nature so calming and rejuvenating. It's like visiting an old friend."

"Exactly! It's not often I find those who share that sentiment." He smiles at her kindly before a woman scurries over.

"Excuse me, Lord Wylington. Lady Wilworth is bickering with your sister again."

"Oh, good heavens. I apologize, but I'll have to tend to this matter before a cat-fight breaks out."

"Of course, of course!"

"It was a pleasure to meet you, Alora." She blushes as he gives her one last charming smile before disappearing behind the hedges.

Looking down at her hands, she smiles to herself before walking over to me, light on her feet.

"Well, how'd I do?"

"You just had a conversation. A very normal conversation. That was not flirting."

"Well, if I don't first start out with conversation to see what he's like, how will I know if I even want to flirt with him?" I furrow my brows at her, looking her up and down as if assessing her.

"You're a curious one, Alora. I just don't know if it's enough fo—"

"Sorry to interrupt," The man returns with two ladies at his heel bickering in hushed whispers. "If I don't have a chance to see you again before you depart, if there's a time you'd want to scour my libraries, please come by anytime."

"I'd like that!" She beams, watching him as he retreats before turning back to me with a self-satisfied smirk on her face.

"You were saying?"

"Right, yes. I suppose this worked out in your favor, but we still need to solidify your interest in him and see if he returns it."

"You could just say you were wrong." She strides past me, her lips thinning as she attempts to hide a grin, and I'm forced to chase after her. Usually, it's me who is chased after.

"Flirting still has its place, you know." I try to keep up with her, my pace usually one of much more leisure. "Could you pause for a moment?" She turns, stopping to look at me as I catch up.

"My goodness woman, for such little legs, you walk fast."

"Just admit that I was right, and you were wrong." She places her hands on her hips, challenging me.

I sigh as if in defeat, leaning in to whisper, my lips hovering over the shell of her ear with a wry smirk.

"Never."

5

Taking me back to my cottage, Eros offered to fly us, but I'm too fearful of heights, as amazing as it might be, so he warns me before teleporting us back.

"Today, progress was made. We continue on this path, and you'll have someone in love with you before spring is up."

"Do you really think so?" I turn to him, wanting to give myself permission to hope, but caution remains the tenant of my heart, and Eros's brows soften slightly before he smiles.

"I will do everything in my power to find a man who will fall madly in love with you. One who would scorch the earth with your name and bow in your reverence." His slender fingers gently brush back a loose lock from my face, my cheeks warming slightly.

"That's quite the romantic talk for someone who doesn't believe in love." I quip, making him laugh.

"Gotta keep up appearances." He winks.

"I'm sure you have much to attend to. I appreciate your help today."

"Oh, yes! I just can't wait to answer the next blubbering buffoon of a man."

"Wait, how do I get in contact with you?"

"Right, just place an offering at the same place you summoned me. I prefer a nice bunch of green grapes soaked in champagne. And luckily enough, you happen to live by this lovely vineyard."

"Did you not see the state of my boots earlier? How am I to afford champagne?" I quirk a brow at him, and he taps a finger to his chin as if in thought.

"Perhaps you should check your icebox." He winks.

"I don't have an icebox."

"You do now." I turn, perhaps a bit too rapidly, towards the kitchen to see a small wooden box with a latched door.

"Wha—" when I turn back to face Ero's, he's gone, leaving behind a faint smell of pink roses. My curiosity goads me to take a peek inside the icebox, unlatching the door to find a shiny bottle of champagne. With my mouth agape, I wrap my fingers around the cold glass bottle, turning it in my hands to find a note attached to the back.

A lovely pleasure as always to spend a day with a beautiful woman. Soak the grapes for approximately eight hours for optimum booziness. Oh, and enjoy a bit for yourself.

Eros

A smile spreads across my lips as I read the note, excited to try champagne for the first time.

He's the biggest flirt I've ever met, but I shouldn't be surprised given he's practically Cupid.

Now, I've seen how champagne has been opened, and it's quite violent, so perhaps I should take it outside lest I break something.

Okay, here goes nothing. Gripping the cork firmly, I pull with all my strength. I jerk back in surprise, giggles falling out of me as the liquid bursts from the bottle in a frothy stream. Once it settles down, I decide to take a swig. Placing the bottle to my lips, I allow the cool, bubbly liquid to coat my tongue and immediately spit it out with a grimace as the remainder of it burns down my throat.

"That's horrid." I glare at the deceitful bottle.

"You're a lot prettier than you taste." I smack my lips together, still tasting the remnants.

I suppose I should go collect the grapes now. Not bothering to grab a lantern with the moon in full tonight, I slide on my slippers and stroll to the vineyard. Plucking the best- looking bunches, I take a few for myself to wash the acrid taste of champagne from my mouth.

With several bunches of plump grapes in the skirts of my nightgown, I pop a few more off the stem, eating them on my way to the back door of the main house. Gilda, the Winton's maid, is usually up at this time of night, so I decide to bribe her with some champagne in exchange for a nice silver bowl to use for the offering.

Rapping my knuckles softly on the back door, Gilda peeks through the glass, her strawberry hair hanging in perfect spirals by her face, a broad smile pulling at her lips when she sees me.

"Alora! Get your arse in here." She rushes me inside. "Is that champagne I see?" She eyes the bottle eagerly.

"It is indeed. I thought I'd offer you a glass if you could perhaps lend me a nice silver bowl?" I arch a brow as I extend the bottle out to her.

"Ain't gotta ask me twice." She wraps her fingers around the bottle's neck, taking a swig with a refreshing *ahh.*

"What are you doing with this anyway—and the grapes?"

"Erm, it's a long story, but the champagne was a

gift." She eyes me suspiciously.

"Alright. I won't prod, but I'll let you do your weird thing." She moves to grab a stack of silver bowls before pausing her reach.

"Wait—you ain't in some sort of cult, are you?" she asks, and I burst out laughing.

"No, I'm in no such thing." She lets out a sigh of relief, grabbing one of the more decorative bowls off the shelf. "I'm just summoning a Greek deity." I can barely contain my grin as her gaze falls to me in disbelief before she chuckles.

"Ah, you're funny."

Little does she know, I'm not joking.

"I'm sorry to hear about what happened between you and that mustached lad." Gilda has never bothered to learn the names of my suitors, as they never stay for long. I nearly laugh at the thought, if only to keep the tears away.

"I don't know what I expected." I sigh, grabbing the cold bowl from her.

"Your mother always had rotten luck with the lads as well." She tsks.

She's not wrong. The only reason I'm here today is because love is not required to bed someone. She always hoped she could break the curse for my sake, but she died before she could.

Gilda's voice brings me back from my thoughts.

"It's not too much to ask for a decent man, Alora. You ain't the problem, sweets." Her eyes soften as she looks at me with sympathy.

"What if I am though—" I set the grapes in the bowl on the counter and take a seat on one of the stools. "I've never felt that pull or desire that others describe when it comes to love. What if I'm broken?" Tears sting my eyes now as I fiddle with the lace of my robe.

"Now you listen to me," Gilda takes my face in her hands. "Love is not only defined by the physical, but also by the heart. You have so much love to give. You are not broken!" She looks firmly into my eyes, letting me know that she speaks true.

"Thank you, Gilda. I know I can always count on you." I smile.

"And don't you forget it."

"Well, I'd best get back. Have to prepare my offering

and all." She narrows her eyes at me, and I can't help but giggle as I leave her with many questions.

Making it back to the cottage, I grab a wide jar from my shelf and pour the bubbling liquid to the rim, the grapes bobbing around. That's when it hits me how absurd this all is. I wonder when I wake up in the morning if I'll find that this has all been a dream, but for now, I enjoy what the day has brought.

6

EROS

Muggsy hops over to greet me when I return home, and I swoop him up, petting his soft fur.

"I haven't forgotten your betrayal, but I love you nonetheless, smooshikins." I hold him up to my cheek, his whiskers tickling me as I place a kiss upon his little head. Radford shakes his leaves, capturing my attention.

"Oh yes, I love you too, Radford." I snap my fingers, a small cloud of rain forming above his leaves, dripping down into the soil for a nice drink of water.

I was just about to plop down in my softest chair when a sparrow flew through the pillars, dropping a seashell into my palm. Ah, Mother has summoned me. With a snap of my fingers, my feet leave my glittering marble to land on a floor swirling with corals and pale blues.

"My son!" Her strawberry blonde hair drapes over her arms and nearly down to her ankles as she walks past all the pillars made of seashells, red roses winding their way around them.

"Thank you for answering that prayer today, my darling. I was buried in summonses today."

"Not a problem. It wasn't the worst prayer I've answered. You actually may be familiar with her, or more so, her ancestors."

"Ah yes, Alora Meadows. Poor darling. When I cursed her ancestor, it was only meant for him, but I'm afraid I didn't gauge my own power at the time, and my fury was raging at that man."

"What happened with him anyway? You never told me the story."

"As you know, many call upon me to wish for true love. Gilford had desperately called upon me for a specific woman who was his heart's desire, and he pleaded with me for a chance to woo her. He sounded so sincere, so I granted him his wish. All seemed well when I found them married and with child. Then, the pig of a man bedded another woman as his wife was in labor and eventually left her and his newborn child for his mistress."

"Ugh, men." I shake my head in disgust.

"I do hope you can aid Alora in breaking her curse. She seems like a lovely girl. I wish curses weren't so hard to break, but you know once I cast one, it's bound tight."

"I know well. Your fury is akin to Father when he wages war. It's one of the things he adores about you. I shall meet with the girl again tomorrow to continue our work. "

"Thank you, my dear boy. I know that love has been lost on you for many moons, but maybe helping this girl break her curse and find true love will make you believe again."

“I’m just doing my job, Mother. You know Psyche crushed any hope or desire for me to ever believe in love for myself.”

“She burned you, but there’s—"

“Mother, if you please, I’d rather not discuss this.” Her face turns down, but her eyes are warm with understanding.

“Of course. I do hope all goes well with Alora.”

“I hope the same.”

Now that Mother has brought up *that* woman, I find myself feeling the pangs of hunger. Perhaps it is heartache, but I refuse to let that be the case, so I will instead drown my sorrows in a big pizza pie and gelato. It’ll be a quick trip to Italy and back, as I’ve got an in with the chef. I mean, he doesn’t know I’m Eros due to my deliciously handsome disguise; I’m just that charming that all the Italian Nonno's love me.

Running my hands over my hair, it smooths out

to a slightly longer blonde, but without the rosy tint. Continuing down the length of my body, my clothes transform until my outfit is complete with a marvelous black waist-coat with coppery blush accents, a blush shirt to match, trousers, and the shiniest boots that could show my reflection. To top it all off, I of course, must have a fancy hat that I flip onto my head with precise trajectory, and a walking stick with gold-carved roses.

"We do look dapper." I say to my reflection as I pose in the mirror. One snap of my fingers later, I'm standing on a stone side street in Gaeta. And yes, this is where I meant to go. Not Naples, as most would believe the dish to originate from, but in Gaeta, the true birthplace of the dish. I would know I was there. Inhaling deeply, I take in the salty air and the freshly yeasted dough being tossed into a blazing stone oven.

Rounding the corner, I spot my little shop, the worn yellow color only adding to its charm, the little flower box I gifted them last time sitting below the window, vibrant and flourishing.

Almost as if he could sense my presence—which is

a mighty hard one to miss, I'll admit, I'm stunning in every way—Luviccio steps outside, beaming as he takes me in.

"Ciao, Amos!" He holds out his arms in greeting, kissing both cheeks. **(And yes, I said my name was Amos. Close enough to the real thing.)**

"Ciao, amico mio. Come stai?" **(Don't worry, I'll translate for you. That means "*Hello, my friend. How are you?*")**

"Lo sto bene, ragazzo mio, e tu?" **(That means "*I'm—*" you know what? I don't want to do this back and forth. You humans must learn more languages. The rest will be automatically translated for you.)**

"I'm good, my boy." He says with the most genuine smile, "Come, come. Let's get you fed."

"The usual? Or are you up for something new?" I'm about to ask for my usual when I stop myself, thinking, begrudgingly, of what Mother brought up earlier. I've been stuck in the same damn rut since Psyche, doing everything as I always do; maybe it's time I change it up a bit.

"You know what? I'll try something new."

"I've got just the pizza." Within a few minutes, he slings the beautiful pie from the oven, placing the masterpiece before me.

"You know, our secret crust."

"Of course." I nod.

"An olive oil and basil pesto base."

"Oh, divine."

"Thinly, thinly sliced potatoes."

"I do love me a spud."

"And to top it all off, parmigiano." **(You should already know that word, and it must be said in Italian. I don't make the rules. Well, some of them I do.)**

With a wide grin, I look to Luviccio in awe of his culinary mastery.

"This sounds like exactly what I need, my friend."

"Now you try." He nods towards the pizza, encouraging me to dig in. Picking up the gorgeously thin slice, I take a bite, always amazed at how perfectly crisp the crust is, not overwhelmed by the toppings. The pesto and olive oil practically infuse themselves into the potatoes that melt in my mouth, the parmigiano adding a slight decadence to the pie. My eyes widen with delight at perhaps the most wonderful pizza I have ever tasted.

"Well?" Luviccio's voice rises in anticipation.

"Luviccio, you have absolutely outdone yourself. My favorite by far." I waste no time in taking a second bite as he shouts in excitement.

"Ah, amore mio. You wonderful boy!" He exclaims with a bright smile. **(Terms of endearment must also be in their native language—it makes me feel more special.)**

"Grazie, grazie, my boy." He kisses the top of my head before telling me to eat up, then disappears into the kitchen, presumably to test out more recipes.

Despite my full belly and my satisfied taste buds, I find I am in need of a sweet treat. I grab myself a hazelnut gelato before popping back into my abode.

Muggsy, who was fast asleep on my chair when I arrived, springs up, now wide awake, his whiskers moving up and down as he sniffs the air.

"You've got too strong a nose for a hare, you know

that. I suppose I'll share." Swiping a small bit of gelato on my finger, I allow Muggsy to lick off his share.

"You spoiled thing." Shaking my body out, my formal attire disappears, replaced with my handsomely chiseled form, free from the restraints of fabric, except for, of course, down there.

Stepping out into my garden, the roses lean slightly towards me as if reaching out. Despite my emotional eating fest and nearly spiraling, today has been one of the better days. I actually feel a slight thrill when I think about helping Alora. She's the only one who has ever thanked me genuinely, and she talks to me as if I am a friend, which I didn't think I would like, but it's quite charming coming from her. Although love betrayed me, I hope to help her find what it means for her.

7

ALORA

The sunrise drifts into my window with an amber glow, gently waking me up in her warm rays. Remembering the events from yesterday, I practically jump out of bed and rush to the kitchen, my bare feet a bit cold on the stone floors. I stop right in the doorframe, my eyes landing on the grapes bathing in champagne, and jump a bit giddily, having confirmed that this is all in fact very real.

Grabbing a mesh cloth, I strain the grapes, collect the champagne into another glass, and nicely place the soaked grapes inside the silver bowl.

I ready myself quickly, tossing on my lavender blue dress, and run a bit of rose oil through my waves to tame them. Grabbing my boots, which Eros had transported back here yesterday, all clean from the muddiness, I lace them up in a rush. I head out the door with a wooden tray holding the offering, and of course, a few bits of bread and berries to give my wildlife friends along the way.

When I reach the ruins, I place the offering at the edge of the broken stairs and step back to await Eros's arrival. After a few moments of shifting back and forth on my heels, I wonder if I need to say something.

"Erm, Eros..." I try to think of what to say next when my thoughts are cut off by a voice coming from behind me.

"So, this is the girl?" I whirl around to see Eros, but he's not alone. A man with similar godlike looks with dark shoulder-length waves, his head adorned with a leafy blackberry crown matching the color of his toga, stands smiling beside him.

"Alora, my love. This is my friend Dionysus." The

god of wine? I mean, I knew other deities existed, but for some reason, seeing two in one place has me a bit frazzled.

He walks forward, placing his palm out. I place my hand in his, a bit hesitantly, and he places a gentle kiss on my knuckles, looking at me through his dark lashes.

"A pleasure to meet you, beautiful." He smiles coyly, and Eros pulls him back by his toga.

"Alright, that's enough, lover boy; she's not yours."

"But she could be." Dionysus sends me a flirty wink, and Eros glares at him like a mother scolding her child.

"I brought your offering." I move aside for Eros to see it, Dionysus peeking over his shoulder in curiosity.

"Alora, you're a dear. You even saved the champagne. Grabbing the glass eloquently as he pops a grape into his mouth, he closes his eyes, savoring it before taking a sip of the champagne.

"Divine." We both turn to Dionysus as he chuckles.

"I'm sorry, you told her to bring you an offering of grapes and champagne?"

"No, I told her to bring an offering of *cham-*

pagne-soaked grapes; and she also happened to save the rest of the liquid. Dionysus shakes his head with a smile.

"What's so funny?" I ask curiously.

"My dear, once a supplicant summons a god or goddess and they agree to aid you, offerings are no longer necessary. You need only just call their name." I turn to Eros, my hands on my hips as I raise a questioning brow.

"It's true. I came because you called for me, not because of the offering. But I wanted champagne grapes, and they taste better when someone else makes them." He shrugs nonchalantly, popping another grape into his mouth. He grins at me as he chews his deceitful treat.

"Unbelievable." I try to feign frustration but can't help the smile that peeks through. "Were you going to make me do this every time?"

"No, I was going to tell you after I finished them all. And hey, you also got a treat out of it."

"I did try a sip, and it was disgusting." I grimace slightly, remembering the bitter taste on my tongue.

Dionysus leans in to add his two cents.

"That's because it wasn't wine. If you come to my vineyard, I can give you the best wine a mortal has ever tasted."

"Dionysus, stuff it back in your pants. She's not going with you." Eros throws one of the grapes at him, which the god of wine catches with surprising ease before popping it into his mouth with a satisfied grin.

"I apologize for him; he wanted to tag along but promised to *behave*." Eros throws back a glare to the other god.

"This is me behaving." Eros ignores him but rolls his eyes, and I chuckle at their banter.

"Anywho. Today, I have the perfect dress for you, and we can work more on your flirtation. Shall we go? I'm sure Muggsy is anticipating your arrival." I take a deep breath, preparing myself for transport.

"Alright, I'm ready." I give him a nod; then one moment, we're in the ruins, the next we are in his home. It takes a minute to collect myself, Muggsy immediately hopping over to rub against my leg.

"Hi, precious!" He chitters as I pick him up, giving

him a kiss.

"Muggsy! You traitor. He does not snuggle up to me that way when I come to visit." Dionysus scoffs, folding his arms across his chest like an upset child.

"She's got a special touch with animals. There are breadcrumbs and dried berries in her pocket for them." My eyes snap up to Eros in surprise.

"How did you know that?"

"I'm a god." He shrugs his shoulders.

"I also brought something for Radford." I look at the fern, his leaves shaking slightly. "I'm sorry for the last time, my friend." I pull out a vial of salt water I made, pouring it into the soil, his leaves perking up.

"What happened last time?" Dionysus asks, amused.

"She upchucked all over the poor fern. He was dreadfully traumatized by the event." Eros says, making me grimace at the memory.

"Fear not, he is quite forgiving, especially with the treat you just gave him." Eros winks at me reassuringly, before walking away, expecting us to follow.

Leading us to the dais and changing area, he takes a

seat, crossing one leg over the other, Dionysus lounging in the chair beside him.

"Now, let's see this dress." Dionysus claps his hands with anticipation. I reluctantly place Muggsy down and step into the box, sliding the drapes closed.

"Ready?" Eros thankfully asks before he performs his clothes-swapping magic.

"Ready." His fingers snap, and my dress is replaced by one of a similar color but with a bit of pastel, the edges laced with a darker trim, and a cream shawl draped around my arms.

"Let's see it then." Dionysus says.

"Don't rush her; if you keep interjecting, you're not coming along." Eros whisper-shouts, and I can sense an eye roll from Dionysus. Pulling back the curtain, I step out and onto the dais to take a look in the mirror.

"My, my, you were right; she is a sight to behold." My eyes find them in the mirror as Eros shoots a glare at his friend, elbowing him.

"Sorry, I'm sorry. I'll shut up now." Dionysus throws his hands up in surrender, but the barest hint of a smirk still lingers at the corner of his mouth.

When Eros turns back to me, our eyes catch in the mirror, and I feel my cheeks heat, averting my gaze down in hopes he doesn't see. He may not have even said that about me. And? So what if he did? He's the god of love. He flirts with everyone.

"Alright, let's go do some flirting!" Dionysus practically jumps up from his seat with a loud clap, taking a swig of wine that appeared in his hand. Eros runs his hands through his hair, the pinkish blonde waves smoothing out, his angel-like form replaced with a black suit adorned with gold embellishments to appear more human.

"My, I do look gorgeous." He smiles at himself in the mirror before turning to Dionysus.

"Your turn." The god of wine opens his mouth to speak, but Eros stops him before he gets the chance.

"Before you argue, yes, you have to change. You're hardly inconspicuous." I chuckle at the god's offended face as he waves a hand down his body, his godly garb replaced with a purple suit so dark, it nearly looks black.

"Alright! Let's go get you fallen in love with."

8

EROS

Facing the doors of the estate, Alora fiddles with her fingers as she musters the nerve to knock.

"You have to knock, beautiful!" As soon as the words leave Dionysus's lips, I turn a sharp glare on him, his hands going up in surrender before he takes a swig from a dark green bottle.

"Put that away and take that dead bush off your head."

"Excuse you, it's a crown." He scoffs, begrudgingly taking it off and vanishing it.

"You can do this Alora; we will be right here with you." I whisper into her ear, taking notice of the gooseflesh that pebbles the skin of her neck. Oh dear, she must be quite nervous.

Exhaling a breath, she steps forward, taking the silver knocker into her fingers and bringing it down on the wood.

The door opens with a surprise briskness that startles Alora, a grayed man looking down at her with an unamused expression.

"Erm, hello. I'm here to see—"

"Lord Wylington, yes. You'll have to come back with the rest of the ladies who are desperate to swoon over Lord—"

"Wallace, I was expecting her; it's alright." Peter swiftly takes the door from his butler, glancing down at Alora apologetically.

"I apologize for him. He's quite used to the ton parading their daughters here and can be a bit of a grump." His lips quirk up into a charming smile, and I can sense Alora's cheeks blushing."

"Right, where's your wine?" Dionysus slides past

Peter, casually walking into the estate before I can catch him. **(Remind me to smite him later for that.)**

"I'm so sorry; these are my chaperones, who seem to have no manners." Alora scowls at Dionysus, who lingers inside, none the wiser.

"Well, are you coming in?" Dionysus turns back to us expectantly.

Peter laughs as he tosses a look back to the god that I regret bringing along now.

"Wine is in the parlor. Please help yourself." Peter gestures towards the grand room, stepping aside to allow us entry.

"I'm so pleased you decided to stop by."

"Thank you for having me. I thought I'd take you up on your offer to see your library." She smiles shyly, fiddling with her fingers again.

"Yes, of course! Shall I get you a drink first?"

"Oh no, thank you. I don't very much like the taste of wine." Judging by Dionysus's grimace as he sips the cherry-red liquid, he's not a fan either, and I have to stifle a chuckle at the face he makes.

"This way to the library, then." Leading the way, we follow Peter to a set of double doors. Alora gasps at the reveal of rows and rows of books lining the wall along with several shelves filling the entirety of the room, leaving only a circle of space at the center where a desk sits.

"This is far beyond what I could have ever imagined." Peter looks at her as she takes it all in, a glint of glee crossing his eyes that makes me falter slightly as I force my brows from furrowing.

"As promised, let me show you my Josephina Mirez collection."

"Yes, please!" She says giddily as he leads her to a far corner shelf.

"We'll be right here the whole time. No funny business." I announce. Alora glares back at me and I send her a wink.

"Our collections are far superior." Dionysus picks up a book, inspecting it. "Have you shown her yours yet?"

"She'd never leave if I did that."

"Then let me show her my library." Dionysus wiggles his eyebrows, and I can tell he's trying to goad me.

"You are a relentless flirt and too much of a player for Alora." I say, trailing a finger along the leather spines as I walk down a row.

"Oh, come on; you've always been my *wing*-man." He nudges me with an elbow, waiting for me to laugh at his pun, but I roll my eyes instead.

"So, I know how much of a flirt you can be. I'm trying to find a man to fall in love with her, not get into her pants. You're the last person I'd consider."

"Hurtful," He places a hand over his heart like he's in pain. "But touché."

I keep a watchful eye on Alora and Peter from over the row of books, watching as she giggles at something he whispers in her ear. I scowl as I carefully watch his hand skimming her waist before he quickly retracts.

"How goes the flirting?" Dionysus appears right beside me, following my line of sight. "Oh, it appears to be going well. Go, Alora!" He smirks as Peter reaches above her to grab a book, a blush fanning across her cheeks. Without thinking, I force the book to fall from Peter's hand, making him clumsily reach for it.

"What was that?" I look over to Dionysus, an amused smile on his face.

"Nothing. Look, it made her find him even more charming." We watch as she bends to help him, their fingers touching over the book like some fairytale moment.

Allowing her to grab it from the floor, she flips to a page, glancing up at Peter with a small smile.

"Shall I read a bit from what is perhaps one of the most beautifully written moments in Josephina Mirez books?"

"Please." Peter leans against a shelf, crossing his arms.

"To love another so fiercely and completely is as freeing as a sparrow. Finding their mate, they hold true, a bond forged for the entirety of their lives,"

I have never heard these words before and find a strange warmth blossoming in my chest at their meaning. I follow Peter's gaze to Alora's lips, about to glare at him from afar until I fall entranced as she continues reading.

"How comforting to be known so, to be seen

through the eyes of the one who is wholly yours. If you shall be granted such a love, hold it close to your heart, lest it fade like a spring mist." I snap myself back to reality, finding Peter inching closer towards Alora. Thinking quickly, I call upon a bird, its wings flapping through the open window, flying right over Peter's head.

Alora shrieks, giggling as they duck down, Peter placing his arms over her short frame.

"I think that's a sparrow." Their cheeks are nearly touching as they look up at the bird flying around.

"Maybe it's a sign." He turns towards her, their eyes meeting, lips inches apart. Right as he's about to close in, a wet pile of poo lands on his shoulder. Alora's hand flies to her mouth as she tries to stifle her laughter, a satisfied smirk rising to my lips as he excuses himself to clean up.

"Eros!" I turn quickly at my name, Dionysus fixing me with a scolding stare. "They were about to kiss, you idiot. Why are you trying to sabotage this date?"

"I don't trust him, alright? There's something off about him." I say, trying to figure out what it is that bothers me so much.

“What do you mean?" Dionysus asks incredulously. "If Alora didn't fancy him, I'd take him for myself. The man is perfect.”

“That’s the problem; he’s *too* perfect.” I scowl, thinking about his lips so close to Alora's.

“How do you mean?” Dionysus steps closer, bending down to whisper.

“Well, for starters, he’s incredibly charming to the point where he could piss his trousers and girls would still swoon.”

Dionysus chuckles like a child, imagining the scene.

“Pay attention!” I slap him lightly on the arm, and he snaps out of his daze.

“Right, sorry. Continue, good sir.” He mock-salutes me.

“He hasn’t tried to be overly handsy with her, but he’s doing those almost touches like you read in the books.”

“Didn’t you say you wanted a gentlemanly man for her? Isn’t him not being handsy a good thing?”

“Usually yes, but I’m struggling to find his flaws,

and he has yet to slip up."

"Eros, are you sure you're not just... *jealous*?" I nearly laugh out loud at that.

"Jealous? Why on Olympus would I be jealous of a mortal man?"

"Hmm, I don't know. Perhaps because he's trying to smooch your girl?"

"Alora? You're joking." I actually laugh out loud at this, but I'm interrupted as we both startle when Alora leans over our shoulders. She's awfully light on her feet.

"What are you two whispering about?" She stands up straight as we turn to look at her, hands on her hips. I can't help the slight smirk on my lips at her trying to appear threatening.

"Oh, you know the usual... the weather." I quip, remembering her first attempt at flirting, and she scoffs.

"Are you making fun of me? I think it's going quite well."

"Oh, it is." Dionysus chuckles to himself.

"Was that you with the bird?" Alora asks, narrowing her eyes on me.

"What? No, that wasn—"

"Because it was quite clever. Getting me into his arms like that." She smiles dreamily.

"Right, yes. I am a mastermind of love." I playfully flick the air.

"Until you made it poo on him. What was that for?" She glares at me.

"Yes, Eros. Whatever was that for?" Dionysus gives me what he thinks is a knowing look, and I roll my eyes.

"Hey, birds are unpredictable creatures. That's not on me." I place my hands up in surrender.

"Now go back out there, scour books, and pretend to be mysterious."

"I *am* mysterious." She whips her dress around her like Count Dracula. **(Yes, I know it wasn't written yet, but that is the best description for it.)**

My smile falters when I turn to Dionysus, who smiles smugly at me like an idiot.

"What now?" I ask, not sure if I even want to know what he's thinking.

"You're an oblivious fool." I don't question him

further on what he means, my ears picking up the voices down the hall.

"You have a visitor, sir, in the parlor."

"Thank you, Wallace. Would you clean off my coat? Damn bird emptied on me."

"Of course, sir."

"Come on." I quietly leave my row, exiting the library with Dionysus cluelessly trailing behind me.

"What are we doing?"

"Eavesdropping on Mister Perfect." I whisper.

Rounding the corner to the parlor, I snap my fingers softly, making Dionysus and me invisible. We watch as Peter approaches a man, who's leaning casually against the fireplace, sipping on some whisky.

"What are you doing here?"

"I heard that the woman from the other day decided to stop by. How's that going?" The man asks, amusement on his face.

"It was going well until a bird interrupted my chance to woo her." Peter says with annoyance.

"So, you think you really have a chance then?"

Dionysus taps me on the shoulder to get my attention.

"What are they talking about?"

"I don't know; we're both listening to the same conversation, now shut up." I wave him off, rolling my eyes as he wanders around the parlor—invisible—making a bottle of wine appear in his hand.

"Yes. That is if I get back to her soon. Why did you come here?" Peter asks quietly, glancing over his shoulder to make sure no one walks in on their conversation.

"I was hoping my money would be well placed, and if it's going as well as you say, I made the right call." The man grins before downing the rest of the whiskey.

This catches Dionysus's attention, already in a wine-drunk stupor. He pops up right in front of the whisky man's face **(Yes, he's still invisible)** looking at him in utter disbelief.

"What the bloody hell does he mean by that?" The drunken god looks back at me in confusion.

"Good luck to you then; I'll take my leave so you can get back to wooing the un-beddable girl." My blood boils at his words, my jaw ticking uncontrollably.

"Oh, he did not just say that about our girl!" Dionysus shouts, about to empty his wine on the man, but I intervene, drawing him back to stand behind Peter.

The man smirks, raising his empty glass to Peter. I'm angry at myself for getting Alora into this incredible mess. When I hear the door close, I remove the glamour that made us invisible.

"So, I was right." Peter jumps back, whirling around to face us.

"What the—" His eyes go wide when he realizes we've heard about his despicable little plan.

"It—it's not what it looks like." Peter's eyes fill with worry.

"Quiet!" I raise my hand, and he immediately falls silent. I inch closer to him, like a predator to prey, anger lit in my eyes.

"You are a skeeving, conniving little—"

"ASSHOLE!" Dionysus shouts from behind me, and I close my eyes for a moment, exhaling a steady breath.

"Excuse him, he gets a little passionate," I tap a finger to my chin as if in thought. "But I do like that word."

"What's going on?" I stiffen when I hear Alora's voice, turning to see her concerned face as she stands in the archway.

"Uh-oh." Dionysus mumbles out, taking a large swig of wine.

"Alora—" Peter starts, but I don't let him finish.

"You!" I point an angry finger at him. "Quiet! Your mouth will never speak her name again."

"Alora, my love, we're leaving." I walk over to her, extending my arm out, and a small sigh of relief escapes me when she grabs it without hesitation, and I lead us out.

"Wait, what happened in there?" She whirls around when she hears a shout to see Dionysus running wobbly down the steps with laughter, a very wet Peter standing in the doorway as dark purple liquid runs down his face, staining his perfectly white shirt.

"What is going on?" She stares wide eyed at the chaotic scene.

"Let's get out of here first, and I'll explain."

9

ALORA

I try to fight the tears that well in my eyes, taking a deep breath as I turn to face the garden as Eros explains what he overheard at the estate.

"Alora, I'm so sorry!"

"It's not your fault." I sniffle, trying to keep my tears at bay. "Did... did I even have a chance?" I hate the desperation that drips from my voice. Eros steps up beside me, his gaze sympathetic.

"Yes, he did find you interesting, but alas, he was a downright buffoon." I chuckle a bit at that. "But I should've sensed his motives earlier."

I sigh, feeling foolish for having gotten caught up in such a man. He just seemed so charming.

"He's a mortal man, and most are good at hiding their true intentions. I don't blame you." I manage a tight-lipped smile.

"Good thing that bird pooed on him then, eh?" Dionysus interjects, making my smile broaden as I wipe away the silent tears.

"Yeah, I guess it is." I laugh. "And thank you for dumping your precious wine on him for me." I walk over to him, his face lighting up when I wrap my arms around him in an embrace.

"Serves him right for calling you un-beddable." His face immediately freezes in shock, realizing he wasn't supposed to tell me the part Eros had so graciously left out.

"Okay, your time is up." Eros waves a hand at him.

"Right, that's fair. Sorry, Alora." Dionysus looks at me pitifully before vanishing. Eros blows out a heavy breath.

"He's a twit."

"But a very loyal twit." I say with a laugh, making Eros's lips turn back up into that charming.

"I'll give him that."

"Did he really call me that?" I shrink into myself, that feeling of brokenness finding its way back into my mind. Maybe there really is something wrong with me; Gilda would have my head if she knew I was thinking this way again.

"I was hoping to spare your feelings on that part." Eros's voice comes out softer than I've heard before.

"I appreciate you helping me, but maybe I'm just not meant to be loved." I turn towards the garden again, not able to look him in the eye. "I've seen those that do not wish for love and find it in someone unexpected, but though I wish for love, it never finds me. Is it so wrong to desire it? It is not the entirety of my being to be in love, for there are many comforts in my life in which I take solace, but the world acts as though I should not want it. They say that perhaps that is when it will find me. But why should I not want it? Why would I not want the kind of love that transcends far beyond the physical?" The tears sting hot down my cheeks, my heart feeling like it's burning to ash.

If soulmates are real, then I'm afraid I do not have one.

"Alora," Eros gently places his fingers under my chin, moving my gaze to his.

"I promised you I would help you find a man that would grovel at your feet, and I shall find you just that."

I stare into his pale blue eyes, searching for hope that my true love is out there. We stay there like that for a moment, and I realize I've been holding my breath when he clears his throat, averting his gaze as he steps back. I wipe at my tears, Eros shining that witty smile at me.

"You know what? I have just the thing to cheer you up. How do you feel about Italian food?"

I gasp as I look out over the cliff of Gaeta, Italy, the bright blue water sparkling in the sun as the waves brush up against the rocks below.

This is beautiful! I grab the railing before me, closing my eyes as I lean over, taking in the salty breeze. When I look at Eros, his eyes are already on me, a softness behind them.

"What?" I ask with a chuckle.

"Nothing; I'm glad to see you smiling. Now, shall we go stuff our faces?"

"Please!"

Coming to a quaint little yellow building along the street, an older Italian man greets us with open arms and a large smile that makes the corners of his eyes crinkle.

"Hello, my boy! Who's the beauty?" **(No, you don't understand Italian now; it is still being translated for you—and yes, I can talk to you outside of my own POV.)**

"This, my friend, is Alora."

"Ahh, Alora. A beautiful name for a beautiful girl, eh?" Luviccio raises his brows at Eros. "What can I get for you today?"

"Two of your finest, the chef special." Eros says in

perfect Italian.

"Yes, yes. I have just the thing." He waves a finger through the air before disappearing inside.

"Shall we sit outside and enjoy the beautiful day?" He looks at me, and I can't help the bright smile that rises on my face. **(Italian food can make any heartache disappear—at least for a while.)**

"Yes, please. This is just stunning." I look out over the cobblestone streets, shops lining the opposite side, waves crashing in the distance.

"Stunning indeed." He grins, leaning back in his chair and crossing his legs.

It doesn't take long for Luviccio to return with our food, the bread perfectly crisp and bubbled with beautiful, charred bits from a stone fire. I'm practically drooling as I watch the steam rolling from the delicacy.

"Enjoy, my friends." Luviccio says in English, smiling kindly before taking his leave.

"Oh my, this smells absolutely delightful. What is it?" Eros delicately rolls a hand through the air, wafting the scent to his nose, inhaling.

"These are what they call Tiella, a double-layered dough filled with various ingredients."

(A modern day—what you call—Calzone, but in triangle form. And don't you dare compare it to a hot pocket or you will get a swift glare from an Italian.)

"The first Tiella is filled with calamari, fresh caught of course, tomatoes, olive oil—only the best, parsley, and a fraction of pepperoncino. The second one is filled with onion, parsley, the finest Gaeta olives, cherry tomatoes, and a bit of red chili for a nice kick." He glances around to make sure no one is looking before snapping his fingers, the Tiella, as he called it, slicing perfectly down the middle of each.

"Here, you must try both, as they are a staple on my visits."

"What is *calamari*?" I test the word on my tongue, picking that one up first. I marvel at the gooey cheese as it stretches half way across the table.

"Oh, right. I forget, you lot aren't quite cultured, **(yet).** Calamari is squid." He watches my face as if he's waiting for me to drop the Tiella in disgust, but this is what I've been missing in life—trying new things, experiencing new ways of life.

I take a large bite, perhaps too large, but I can't find it in myself to regret it as the flavors dance on my taste buds, the tender calamari mixing wonderfully with the tomatoes. It's not as fishy as I was expecting.

"Ohmmy gshhh." I mumble out through a mouthful of Tiella, forgetting my etiquette; but I couldn't be bothered to care at this moment. I look up at Eros when he chuckles to find an amused grin on his face.

"I forget how cute humans can be when they experience things for the first time. Like little chicks learning how to walk." I finish chewing, washing the bite down with some sparkling juice.

"Did you just compare me to a chick?"

"Yes, but a cute chick. Now try the next one; I must know your reaction."

He watches carefully as I bite into the second Tiella, leaning closer in anticipation as he awaits my judgement. My eyes go wide with shock at the multitude of flavors that this singular dish contains and how they all blend so harmoniously.

"These are bloody fantastic." I shout a bit loudly, forgetting myself once again, and Eros laughs delightedly. When I notice him staring, lips pressed together as if to suppress a grin, I take another sip of the juice before asking what he's staring at.

"You, you've just got a bit of—here," he leans over, and before I can think to be embarrassed, he swipes the incredibly soft pad of his thumb gently beneath my bottom lip, my body still as I watch him. "You had a bit of sauce, my love."

"Oh dear, I truly have forgotten myself. I'm sorry." I chuckle under my breath, a blush fanning across my cheeks.

"Fret not, love. I find it truly charming to see a lady eating ravenously." A flirty glint shines in his eyes as he sends me that signature smirk, and I have to hold back an eye roll. "And why do you apologize so often? You needn't apologize for enjoying yourself."

"Well—I—I don't know. I guess it's just instinct." I guess I never realized it before, and I'm not quite sure why it is that I say it so often.

(She's afraid of conflict and doesn't realize she's

apologizing for simply existing. Rubbish societal standards and all—and yes, I just called her out in her own POV.)

"Well, you needn't apologize so much with me."

"Right, sorr—" I immediately stop myself from wanting to apologize for apologizing—again, when he looks at me with a quirked brow.

"Okay." I say with as much confidence as I can muster.

"There we go." He smiles approvingly. "Now you're getting it." I can't help but smile at the positive reinforcement. "Now," he leans in over the table with a grin, "Shall we grab dessert?"

He takes me to a small, canopied cart where a man sits on a bicycle attached to the end, a cold compartment with gelatos of all kinds sitting in metal bins inside. I decide to go for the hazelnut flavor and nearly lose my sense of self once again when I taste the decadent treat.

"How do you ever leave this place?" I glance over to Eros where he—very irritatingly—eats his pistachio gelato with the utmost sophistication as I chase the melting drops on the cone with my tongue.

"Oh, darling. There are many more places rich in history and delicious foods that would blow your mind. Don't tell the Italians..." he leans down to whisper. "But Falasteen has *the best* olive oil. Their olive trees are ancient, giving the oil a rich and robust taste."

"How I wish to see the world someday." I sigh a little to myself, taking in all the beauty as we walk near the cliffside, wishing this was my everyday.

"And perhaps you shall one day. If we can only find you a rich man." As if we summoned just that, a very handsome Italian man in no doubt, very expensive clothes, smirks at me and walks over.

"Hello, beautiful." He says in a low romantic tone, kissing my hand in greeting, and I blush at the attention.

"No, absolutely not! Off you go." Eros states firmly,

shooing off the man.

“Wha—why did you do that?” I ask with furrowed brows.

“These kinds of men may be handsome and know how to romance you, but trust me, I’ve experienced enough Italian men to know the ones who are up to no good.”

"Alright." I say, pouting a little, knowing Eros enough to trust him, but disappointed that it's always the same kind of man that would break my heart given the chance.

“It’s getting late back in England, so we best get back. Are you ready?” Eros asks, extending a graceful hand to me.

“Yes, I don’t think I’ll vomit on poor Radford anymore.” That earns a hearty chuckle from him.

One snap of his fingers later, and we’re standing in the dewy evening grass by my cottage door.

“Alright, we will reconvene tomorrow and formulate a new and even better plan.” He turns on his heel, raising his hand, about to blip away.

“Wait—Eros!” I step forward, instinctively reaching

out for his arm, but drop my hand before I touch him.

"Yes, love?" He turns, his features even more striking illuminated by the moonlight.

"Thank you for tonight. And for all you've been doing to help my plight. I truly appreciate what you did for me today." His eyes soften as he looks down at me, his smile true and genuine.

"Of course, Alora. You are deserving of the very best. Do remember that." He gives me one more reassuring smile before he disappears right before me.

10

EROS

"Good, you're back."

"What the—" I whirl around to find Dionysus lounging in my chair with Muggsy and sigh, rubbing a couple fingers to my temple.

"Dionysus, what are you doing here?" I walk over to my bar, which is quite the delicious marble luxury, and pour out something a little stronger than wine.

"I had to check in on how our little human is doing. I'm invested now." He walks over while obnoxiously stroking Muggsy, anticipating an answer.

"Stop calling her *our* human." I take a rather large swig of my drink.

"Ahh—right, right. Because she's only *your* human." He's trying to get under my skin, and I swear, if I did not actually consider him a friend, I'd smite him if I could.

"You know you've become a real thorn in my side. Give me back my hare." I steal Muggsy away from him, needing his comfort for myself, taking a seat in my comfy chair.

"Oh, you know you love the pain." He jests. My, sometimes I do wonder why I am friends with him.

"And she's just *a* human." I continue trying to end this conversation.

"Ahmmm." He hums as if he knows something I don't—like he doesn't believe me, and I do not have the energy to argue with him right now.

Once I find her the love of her life, we shall go our separate ways, and I shall live on eternally as she grows old with her love.

"You never answered me. How is she? I really do

quite like her. I haven't had as much fun as I did this afternoon in Olympus knows how long."

"She's doing better. I do think our little trip helped perk her up, but she's also just saving face from the disappointment of her date with that wretched man." I grimace even thinking about him.

"Ooh can we curse him? Perhaps give him never-ending facial hair that grows back immediately after shaving, or maybe we can make him bald by thirty—ooh ohh no, what if we give him a wedgie for the rest of his days?" Dionysus taps his fingertips together excitedly.

"That would be quite funny, as he'd have no idea what to call his quandary, since that word hasn't been coined yet." I can't help the smile that comes as I imagine doing all of these things before snapping out of my stupor.

"No, no. Alora would not want that. She's too kind to curse another, given her situation." I wave away the thoughts.

"And since when do you do as a human likes?" I open my mouth to speak but find myself curious. I'm not quite sure why I cater to Alora's whims. She is quite charming for a human—obviously; Dionysus can't shut his trap about her.

"I suppose I am quite fond of her. I'd think us good friends in another life." Dionysus lets out a long sigh, pinching the bridge of his nose.

"You, clueless oaf." He mumbles under his breath, barely audible, but he'd know I'd hear with our godly hearing.

"Name-calling, now, are we? That's what we've resorted to?"

"Yes! Especially when my best friend is being an insolent fool, but I shall leave you to discover things on your own." He stands. Stealing my glass from me, he downs the rest of the alcohol before lifting a hand, about to transport away.

"Discover what?" He pauses mid-snap, looking at me over his shoulder with a lighthearted scoff.

"You're such an idiot." Then he's gone in a blink, leaving me dumbfounded and with an empty glass. Dionysus is always full of nonsensical thoughts. **(Don't you dare look at me that way, reader. I**

could curse you right now. I assure you, Dionysus is the fool.)

The next morning, I wake up invigorated, having high hopes of figuring out a new plan with Alora. I may or may not like the prolonged affair, as it keeps me from the blubbering, snotty humans that I usually have to deal with.

I think that Muggsy would appreciate another visit from who is apparently now his favorite—at least I still have you Radford, right? I look to the fern, who definitely is perhaps still a bit scarred from being puked on.

"There, there, my friend. She'll never hurt you again." His leaves wave softly as if in a breeze—that means he's grateful.

Teleporting to her door, which happened to be opening at the same time I appeared, she jumps back startled, clasping a hand over her heart.

"Good heavens. I wasn't expecting you there."

"Apologies, but I do find startled humans quite cute."

"Of course you do." She chuckles. "So, what's on the schedule for today?"

"Well, Muggsy is having withdrawals from you, so

we must tend to that matter first."

"Hm, I think he likes me more now." She walks past me with a gloating smirk.

"A blasted traitor, he is. I think even Dionysus likes you more than me at this point as well." She turns back to look at me, the morning sun rays catching her irises just right, the golden flecks within them sparkling.

"Don't worry, you're still my favorite god." Her lips quirk up, and a little pair of wings beat in my chest.

"Oh, I never doubted that." I stride up beside her as she walks into the forest, her hand digging into her apron pocket for the crumbs and berries.

"You're certain? Because yesterday you seemed quite annoyed anytime Dionysus interacted with me." She chuckles as she bends down, reaching a hand-full of breadcrumbs to a few forest critters.

"Why does everyone seem to question me lately?"

"What else have you been questioned about?" She asks with a laugh.

"Hmm?" I immediately regret even stating that, given the implications Dionysus made last night.

Dreadfully wrong, he was.

"Oh, nothing. You know, the god of wine, being his usual drunkard self, insisted on peppering me with nonsensical questions." I wave a nonchalant hand through the air.

"Do you want to try?" She looks up at me with those doe-like eyes before nodding her head, gesturing towards the waiting animals. I hold my palm out, and as she places a few crumbs and berries into my hand, her fingers brush against my skin, sending a weird shock through me. Humans are so full of static electricity.

"Hello, little ones. It's my turn to steal your love away from Alora." I toss a glance back at her as she looks down at me, chuckling.

I nearly giggle like a child as the tiny noses and whiskers tickle my hand, not having done such a mundane task in ages. Squatting down beside me, she holds her hand out once again, a few of the creatures skittering over to her.

"I think they still like me more." She jests, and I watch her as the corners of her eyes crinkle in delight, the small dimple that's barely noticeable unless you pay attention, coming out as she grins with glee.

A beam of light filters through the trees, bathing her in its ethereal glow, and I find myself entranced until a bird flies down, swooping over our heads. Alora immediately stands, sheltering her head with her arms.

"I swear, Eros, if you make this one poo on me—" She tracks the bird as it flies above us. I stand, zeroing in on the creature, my eyes lingering on the flap of its wings as I notice the kind... *a sparrow*. Shaking my head and coming back to reality, I chuckle at her apprehension.

"I assure you, this one won't poo on you, my love." Hesitantly, she brings her arms down as she watches the bird.

"Alright, I'm trusting you." She stands in full, and the sparrow flaps down gently to her. She extends out her hand, the little feet wrapping around her fingers, and she giggles, a warmth spreading throughout my chest at the sound.

"See, harmless."

"He's so beautiful." She gently strokes his feathers,

the bird chirping softly before flying away towards the sky.

"Shall we get you to Muggsy? Mustn't keep him waiting—he can get quite the temper."

"Right, right. Good thing I have some treats to butter him up."

"What, no treat for me?" I tease.

"Well, you can take some grapes from the vineyard."

"I'm just messing with you. You're treat enough." I send a playful wink at her, and she shakes her head at me with a smile.

Snapping my fingers, our feet leave the forest floor to stand on my glittering marble.

"Muggsy!" Alora shouts excitedly as the hare jumps over to her and into her arms.

"You sweet thing, I brought you a treat. She holds out some dried strawberry tops, his favorite, and he nibbles away at them contentedly.

"Alrighty! What outfit shall we go for today, darling?"

"Erm, what's your plan for me today?"

"Well, there is a nice art museum showing this afternoon where I'm sure many potential suitors will be. So we doll you up, scope out the scene, pick your ideal man, and then give it a go." Her brows crease, lips thinning as she continues to feed Muggsy.

"I know what you're thinking, but don't give up just yet, hmm?" I walk over to her, placing a finger beneath her chin, gently moving her until she's looking at me, and she can't help but smile softly.

"Still trust me?" I look down at her with a sincere smile.

"Yes." She whispers.

"Okay, then. Let's get you dressed." I clap my hands, the changing room appearing near the dais. Once she's inside, I snap my fingers, a new outfit appearing on her.

"Eros!" She shouts with scorn, but she's never believable when she pretends to be mad at me, and I smile to myself at the thought.

Stepping out from the curtain, I bend over in laughter as she stands there with a glare. The dress is a wide, boxy thing appearing like drapes of a tent, the top half striped with red and white, little animals sitting along the waistline as a trapeze artist dangles down the middle of the two drapes. But what really makes it is atop her head full of the biggest spiral curls, is a Ferris wheel that's actively spinning.

"Really?" Her tongue pokes the inside of her cheek as she places her hands on her hips.

"What? We're going to an art museum, and you're an art form." I chuckle, a smile cracking through her annoyed façade. "I mean, you have to admit, it's quite impressive." She comes to stand in the middle of the dais, taking it all in with surprise written all over her face.

"Okay, fine. It is quite spectacular, but not what I want to go for."

"Alright, alright. Back in you go." I flick my hands at her, shooing her inside.

With another snap, her attire changes once more, hopefully with her approval this time. Walking out in a stunning dress of blush pink, the skirt a satin material with a sheer veil of fabric cascading over it, the sleeves puffing out slightly, looking like petals of a flower that have been intricately placed, her long dark waves forming a stunning up-do with soft curls framing her face.

"Exquisite." I whisper almost breathlessly, a fondness warming me at seeing her in my color. She twirls around, taking a look at herself in the mirrors.

"Wow, it's beautiful." She remarks with a gentle smile at herself.

"Indeed." I say as I take her in.

"Wow, a real beauty, she is." I jump, **(imperceptibly to you humans, but very noticeable to Dionysus, who has just appeared behind me—the twit).**

"Why, thank you!" She curtsies, and Dionysus swiftly strides over to her, grasping her hand to lead her in a dreadfully inaccurate dance. But I can't help the grin that rises on my lips as they both move around in laughter.

"These mortal men don't deserve you." Dionysus says as he extends their bodies apart so he can look at her.

"Try telling them that." She laughs, but I can see the glint of pain crossing her eyes.

"Right, so when do we leave?"

"*You—*" I stand, sauntering over to them. "Are not coming along. You're a nuisance, and this must go smoothly for Alora." Dionysus leans in close to me, speaking under his breath.

"Ahh right, you want alone time with her." He looks at me with a wink as I blink at him, unamused.

"You're relentless. She needs alone time with a man who isn't the scum of the earth." I say back, keeping my voice low, grateful Alora is distracted playing with Muggsy. Oh, humans are so cute with how easily they lose focus.

"Time for the party?" She looks over at us, and I perk up, acting like we weren't just speaking of her.

"It is indeed." I extend my arm out, Alora joining hers in mine.

"I'll just be here, I guess... and wait until you return with my updates." Dionysus lets out an exaggerated sigh before summoning a tray of grapes. I roll my eyes as Alora chuckles before I snap my fingers, arriving at the front steps of the art museum.

11

ALORA

"This place is enormous." I gasp, taking in the large cream-colored building with hand-carved pillars lining the length of it.

"Wait till you see the inside." Eros leans down to speak in my ear as loads of people with loud chatter pass us by.

"Shall we?" He grins down at me, waiting for my go-ahead. Shaking off my nerves, I smile back and nod.

Right upon entering, there's a sculpture of a waterfall, so incredibly detailed, it looks as though real water has been frozen in time.

"Stunning, isn't it?" I nod, my mouth slightly agape as I stare transfixed by the piece. Without thinking, my hand extends out, fingers nearly brushing the stream of water when someone shouts, startling me back.

"Hey! No touching the art pieces!" A man with slicked-back dark hair, a curled mustache, and a pressed suit, walks over towards us, his pocket embroidered with the name Cecil. His face is pinched as he waggles a finger at me, and a rush of embarrassment fills my chest, my cheeks heating up as a few heads turn our way.

"Have you never been to an art show before? No touching!" He scolds.

"I—I haven't, I'm sorry." I say in a breathless rush, and Eros steps forward before the man can say anything more.

"You do not talk to women that way, you blasted mortal." The man's brows furrow slightly in confusion, but before he can think about the insult further, Eros continues.

"This is her very first art experience, and I will not

have it tainted by a rat-faced man with enough gel in his hair to be as hard as one of these sculptures, who also cannot respectfully state a rule." Cecil's face reddens like a ripened tomato. "And you know what? She can touch this piece if she likes. I'm buying it, so it is now my property."

"B—but—" Cecil is stunned into silence, and I can tell he's afraid to speak further. "These pieces aren't for sale." He clears his throat, pulling down on the bottom of his jacket in an attempt to collect himself.

Just then, a woman in a lavish gown with greying blonde hair placed in perfect curls atop her head, saunters over. The name *Matilda Merrison*—the same name as the museum—is stitched onto the top of her bodice.

"Excuse me, beautiful lady." Eros greets her, and a flattered smile tugs at her lips.

"Why, hello. How can I assist you?"

"You're the matron of this establishment, correct?"

"I am indeed."

"My name is Amos Aetos, and I'd like to make a considerable donation to this museum as well as purchase this lovely statue."

"Oh, my! Yes, we shall make the arrangements right away." She claps her hands together delightedly.

"You're a dear. Thank you." He delicately takes her hand in his, kissing the tops of her glove as she blushes.

"Yes! Well, thank you very much for your donation." She says breathily before disappearing back into the crowd. Eros returns his daggered glare to the greasy man.

"That's settled then, isn't it? Alora, touch the sculpture as much as you like, my love." Cecil fixes his pointed scowl at us before walking away with in a huff of frustration.

"That was spectacular." I can't help the chuckle that escapes me as Eros turns back to me.

"Nobody is going to yell at you like that and get away with it." He smiles down at me, and now my cheeks are hot for a different reason. "Now, let's find you a man."

12

EROS

"Shall we walk around and see who catches your eye?"

"You'll have to use your super hearing to listen in on conversations so I can see what kind of person they are." Right, Alora can admire aesthetics, but that's not what solidifies it with her.

"Of course, my love." We come to a group of men looking upon a painting of Demeter assisting a woman in a field of barren crops. She's always been such a lovely goddess.

"How about any of them?" She leans in, whispering. I cue my ears into their conversation, immediately appalled by their inappropriate comments made about the women's bodies.

(Men who are reading this, pay attention. This is not what will get you a woman. You must cherish the soft and strong nature of women without focusing so much on appearance or resorting to slander.)

"So?" Alora glances up at me, bringing me back from their abhorrent conversation.

"Not a single one of them is good enough for you, my love. Moving on."

She glances around, trying to pay attention to how each man is viewing the art before finally landing on one standing by himself, hands clasped behind his back as he admires a painting of a woman frolicking through wildflowers.

"What about him?" She points to a man with dark brown skin and curly hair, who could be the very definition of tall, dark, and handsome.

"I guess you'll have to talk to him and find out if

he's someone you'd like to flirt with." I wink down at her and she smiles sheepishly. Nervously, she steps forward, coming to stand beside the man.

"It's a beautiful painting, isn't it?" She asks, and he turns to her with a soft smile.

"Indeed. She looks so carefree and happy. At times I wish I could do exactly as she is."

"Everyone needs a good field frolic from time to time." She chuckles, making his smile grow wider, and a strange tightness grips my chest, but I shake it away.

"It seems like great medicine, but unfortunately, it is not proper for a man to traipse around in a field of flowers."

"Societal norms do like to put a damper on fun, don't they?"

"I suppose so. Maybe I'll be brave enough to defy them someday... and perhaps we could frolic together?" He glances at her with his golden-brown eyes, her cheeks heating up as she grins.

(Well, this is going rather well, don't you think? Yes, I am talking to you, reader. Please catch up. This is much better than the cummer-

bund situation.)

"Have you any plans for Saturday evening?" The man asks. "Because there is this sort of soiree I am to go to, and I thought it might be lovely to go with an even lovelier guest."

Oh, he's good. I watch suspiciously, every so often pretending to admire a painting to blend in.

"I'd very much like that." She grins, looking down as she fiddles with the fabric of her dress. "Wait, you were inviting me, right? Oh gosh, I should've asked if that's what you meant." Her blush quickly turns to a flush of embarrassment, and the man just laughs, charmed by her. *Of course, he is—who wouldn't be by that adorable little nose scrunch she does when she's nervous.*

"I suppose I should introduce myself. Avin Oakton. And who might the beautiful lady I've been talking to be?" He extends his hand out with a slight bow, Alora delicately placing her fingers over his.

"A pleasure, Avin. I'm Alora Meadows." He places a chaste kiss on the top of her hand, grinning up at her through his lashes. I almost roll my eyes at how sickeningly sweet it is when I remember I should be happy for how well this is going.

"I shall see you soon, Alora Meadows."

"You shall." She smiles brightly, curtsying. When he's no longer in sight, she rushes over to me with a giddy glee.

"Did you see that? It went well, don't you agree?" She grabs onto my arm excitedly with both hands.

"It did. You have improved, my love. I'm quite proud." She beams up at me, a faint blush returning to her cheeks, and this time, that weird flutter of wings returns to my chest. It must be from their flirtation lingering in the air.

13

ALORA

Returning home with a bit of a spring to my step from how well it went at the museum, I nearly forget that I'm to have dinner this evening with Mr. and Mrs. Winton, and I'm cooking.

I rush to the main house, Gilda graciously helping me chop some veggies. She's always been so great to me, but we rarely see each other unless I'm at the main house for dinner or I sneak over in the late evenings, so prepping is the most time we get to catch up.

"So, how has it been over here?" I ask her as I stir the

gravy for the roast chicken.

"The Mr. and Mrs. have been out a lot lately, so the workload has been light these days."

"That must be nice. I hope you're using some of the time to take care of yourself."

"Oh, I may have used a fancy bath soap here and there." She says, and we both chuckle.

"Please tell me they aren't planning on setting me up this evening. I don't think I have it in me to feign interest right now." She doesn't answer right away, turning her back on me as she pretends to grab a few more carrots.

"Gilda?" I elongate the last vowel.

"Well, they may have found a man and invited him over for dinner to meet you." She glances at me, biting off a chunk of carrot.

"Ugh. Why can't they just let it be?" I sigh.

"I suppose they want you to be taken care of. But these men ain't shite."

"Gilda!" I say incredulously, but I can't help but laugh as she cracks a wide grin.

"Okay, I suppose I'll just have to get through dinner

and hope he's not horrible."

"Good luck with that, sweet."

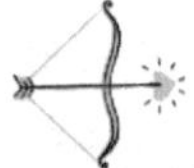

After a couple hours of letting things stew and simmer, I rush back to my cottage as Gilda dishes out the meal so I can clean up and change.

I glance at myself in the mirror, my waves a bit frizzed from standing over the stove, so I take a bit of rose oil and smooth out the strays.

I let out a heavy breath, finding the last bit of courage I have to face this dinner, and head out the door.

To my surprise, the man is already here, sitting with Mr. and Mrs. Winton in the parlor. Noticing me, he stands and bows slightly.

"Alora, dear. We have a dinner guest this evening." She gestures to the man, his full blonde hair lying in a swoop on his head, his frame tall and a bit lanky. When he smiles at me, his green eyes linger far too long on my chest. I roll my eyes internally, already annoyed by him and I don't even know his name yet.

"This is Bernath Tinswell."

"Oh, you're much... *curvier* than I was imagining." He mumbles to himself, but it's clear enough that we all heard. I pinch my brows together as I stare at him. Mrs. Winton clears her throat, her gaze bouncing between us nervously.

"We've told Bernath here about how much you love animals. Perhaps you both could take a lovely nature stroll together sometime." She says with a smile, attempting to salvage the situation.

Like I would care for him to be around my precious animals or be near-alone with him in the woods; no thank you!

"Mmm, yes. I've heard much about you." He eyes me up and down, his tone unimpressed.

"Oh. Have you?" I glance at Mrs. Winton, and she subtly ticks her head towards him as if to say, *just please try*.

"Right, it's a pleasure to meet you as well, Bernath." i say, forcing a smile to my face.

“Shall we eat?” Mr. Winton leads us to the dining room. Gilda wheels out a cart full of plates, stopping a bit longer behind my chair before placing my meal down.

“Well, this one’s a twit, much like the rest, eh?” She whispers, and I have to refrain from chuckling.

“So, you mentioned you’re a mortician,” Mrs. Winton inquires and my eyes go wide as I bite into a piece of chicken, hoping he doesn’t go into detail lest I lose my appetite. Although, if I were to upchuck on him, it’d be sure to send him running.

“I am, yes. It’s quite peaceful working with the dead rather than the living.” They chuckle, nodding in agreement.

"Mm, I bet." Mr. Winton says agreeingly, an awkward tension lingering in the air.

“I’ve actually found it a bit difficult to get the formaldehyde smell from my hair—not a scent that the ladies admire.” Bernath chuckles.

Right, because it’s only the smell that sways them off, is what I wish I could say. instead, I take a bite of potato and pretend to find him funny.

“But, Alora, you don’t strike me as a woman in a position to worry about such trivial things.” His lips curve into a patronizing smile, and I narrow my eyes at him.

What is that supposed to mean?

Sensing the tension, Mr. Winton speaks into the thick silence.

“Erm, perhaps you could tell us how one comes into the mortuary business?” He graciously moves the conversation away from me.

“Well," Bernath shifts his condescending gaze off of me. "I suppose it’s just the family business. I never imagined I’d go into it. I actually want to be a politician.”

Oh gods! Where did they find this man?

"My, what an aspiration!" Mrs. Winton beams delightedly.

“So, tell me, Alora. Have you ever seen a dead body?” My hand freezes on the stem of my glass at his question, my mind conjuring up the images of my mother, her body still and lifeless in her coffin. My toes wiggle absentmindedly in the worn leather boots that are all that remain of her.

"Yes, I have." I say flatly, taking a long drink of the wine—not even liking its taste—but needing the distraction of the bitter sting of it down my throat. Mr. and Mrs. Winton peer at me awkwardly, before averting their gaze to their plates. "If you'll please excuse me, I need to freshen up." I strain a smile.

"Of course, dear." Mrs. Winton sends a sympathetic look my way as I stand from the table.

Escaping to the nearest corridor, I let out a frustrated sigh.

"Gods, Eros—if you can hear me, please help get me out of this nightmare!" I look up, for a reason I'm not sure of—is Olympus up or somewhere else entirely?

"You called?" That low voice whispers in my ear, startling me from my thoughts as I whirl around to face none other than the god himself.

"Thank gods you heard me. Please, please help me out of this atrocious mess! They have tried to set me up with this mortician who—"

"Say no more..." He holds up a hand, a devious smile spreading across his lips before he disappears.

Standing there confused and alone, my eyes wander around to see if he'll pop up again.

"Eros? So, are you helping?" Just as I ask the question, there's a knock at the door.

Gilda swings it open, gasping loudly.

"My, my! Who are *you*?" I round the corner to see her fanning herself with a hand and—Eros; he stands in the doorway in a fine suit and a gaudy walking stick, his waves slicked nicely on his head, and my mouth drops open.

"Hello, lovely. I am here for Alora."

14

EROS

"Ah, hello love." I say to Alora when she steps out from the corridor, her eyes roaming over the entirety of me with curiosity.

"Well, who might this be?" Mr. Winton asks as they all migrate to the foyer.

"Oh, how rude of me to not properly introduce myself. I'm Amos, Amos Aetos. I am courting the lovely Alora, here." My eyes flick to her, her cheeks flushing a delicious pink before she looks away.

"Alora, dear. You didn't tell us you had a suitor."

Mrs. Winton speaks, a hand over her heart as she smiles joyfully.

"I—erm, well, I—"

"You know how courting goes. I believe she wanted to see where things went before she announced that we were courting." She glances at me with a nervous expression, but I can tell she's grateful for my intervention.

"Right, yes. You know all those previous lousy suitor encounters I've had." She chuckles breathlessly.

"Mmm yes, most unfortunate." Mrs. Winton agrees before striding over to where I stand at the door. "Well, do come in, please."

The mortician side-eyes me as I waltz past him, following Mrs. Winton to the table. Alora sits down beside me, her fingers rubbing together anxiously.

"So, I suppose there's a bit of competition then for Alora's hand." The mortician speaks with a bitter edge.

"Oh, not at all. Alora is not some prize to be won." I eye him from over the rim of my glass as I sip on the red wine, his eyes narrowing. Alora glances at me with softened eyes, and I wonder if she truly has never been treated with such basic respect that each woman deserves. **(Typical men, pshh.)**

"Of course not. I mean... it is up to the lady I suppose." Bernath clears his throat awkwardly, shifting in his seat as he tries to recover.

"What do you do for a living, Amos?" Mrs. Winton asks with a smile.

"I work in the realms of the heart." I raise my brows at Alora, making her chuckle.

"Oh, a heart surgeon? How fantastic!" Mrs. Winton claps excitedly.

"I—I know a thing or two about the heart as well..." Bernath chimes in, obviously desperate to impress. "Did you know, during rigor mortis, the heart stiffens, almost making it look enlarged?" He nods, pleased with himself as the rest of us grimace.

"Ah yes, wonderful dinner conversation." I smirk at Bernath and take another sip of wine, Alora trying to hide her grin. He glares daggers at me, as if that would affect a god.

For the rest of dinner, he attempts to seem more

intriguing but can't catch the hint that no one wants the gruesome details of an autopsy as they eat their chicken.

Finishing up dessert, we move to retire in the parlor, but Mr. and Mrs. Winton are so enthralled by my captivating persona that they trap me in conversation, Alora and Bernath having already exited the room. Being the ever-so-amazing god that I am, I tune my ears into their conversation while continuing to listen to the older couple.

"There's no way that man has any real interest in you." Bernath sneers, and my jaw clenches at this absurd man. *"I am your best chance."*

"What does that mean?" Alora asks incredulously.

"Well, you're not exactly the most desirable woman, and word has gotten around that... consummation won't be easy with you." She scoffs in disbelief at his brazen words, but before she can say anything, I saunter over as Gilda so graciously takes the Winton's attention.

"Listen here, you sorry sack of insecure masculinity..." Bernath's eyes blow wide, and he looks around in shock. "You would be most lucky for Alora to even look your way, and if you're as daft as you seemed during dinner, let me make it clear. You will not talk to her like that, or any woman for that matter, ever again. And as for my interest in Alora, you may be afraid of a little curve and a relationship beyond the physical, but a real man is not." I wrap my arm around Alora's waist, not missing the pink that rushes to her cheeks and down her neck and... *oh, gods; eyes back up, Eros.*

"Never mind," Bernath spits out. "I have many other women to court." With that, he makes his exit.

Some men never learn.

"Drinks, anyone?" Mrs. Winton's voice startles Alora, and she quickly steps away from me, brushing a wave behind her ear. "Oh, where has Bernath gone?" She looks around the room for him.

"He mentioned something about emergency mortuary business." I make up a story for the poor excuse of a man.

"Erm, I'm actually quite tired." Alora says. "And Amos here mentioned he has a *surgery* tomorrow." She glances at me, signaling for me to play along.

"Yes, right! I have a dreadfully early day tomorrow. But thank you kindly for dinner." I bow, placing a kiss on Mrs. Winton's hand.

"Oh, of course, dear. We're just so happy Alora has found a suitor."

"Good night, *Amos.*"

"See you soon, my love." I whisper, winking at her before disappearing out the door.

"Eros?" Alora whispers as soon as she's far enough away from the house. She bumps into my solid frame when she turns around with a cute little "ope."

"That was mighty fun, I must say." I smirk down at her.

"Thank you for getting me out of that disaster." She says, turning on her heel towards her cottage.

"Gods woman, you and your little legs move far too quickly." She chuckles as I stride up beside her.

"You know." She stops abruptly, turning back to me

again with a finger in the air. "I think some Muggsy snuggles are in order."

"Oh, I know he'd adore his Alora snuggles. I'm still quite jealous, you know." I bring my fingers up to snap, pausing when she stops me.

"Wait! Let me prepare." She inhales a deep breath.

"Oh, yes. Mustn't traumatize poor Radford again. He's come to like you."

She breathes out in a chuckle, the sounds making that tiny pair of wings flap again.

"Okay, I'm ready." With her approval, I snap, our feet landing in the center of my garden in a puff of rosy glitter, the place aglow with warm lantern light. She places her hands out to steady herself, relieved that the contents of her stomach remain inside.

"Hey, I think I'm getting the hang of this magical travel." She beams, clapping her hands together.

"Indeed, you are. I'm very proud." I wink, and her cheeks warm at the praise.

Muggsy—the traitor—jumps over to Alora from where he was resting on a chair, chittering in excitement.

"Hello, my sweet friend! You make everything better." She hugs him tightly to her chest.

"I'm sorry you had to deal with such a rotten man—if he can even be called one." I glance at her in sympathy as I trace a finger along a rosebush.

"You made the evening enjoyable. So, thank you for the rescue. I don't think I could've stood to deal with him again." She laughs half-heartedly, not able to fully hide the hurt.

"Even gods have their fair share of rotten romance." I say, and she looks at me in surprise.

"Really?"

"Do you remember when I told you I no longer believe in love?"

"Yes, you seemed badly scorned by it."

"Very much so." I sigh, looking off into the night sky that swirls like a painting in blues and purples, speckled with glimmering stars. "A long time ago, and I mean a very long time ago, I know I look quite well for my age..." I glance back at her with a smirk, earning a small chuckle. "I was in love. Madly, truly, and deeply head over heels, the only time I had been so."

"What happened?" Her gentle eyes follow me as I wander through the garden.

"She was stunning in every way, enrapturing me from the very moment I saw her. Her name was Psyche, and her beauty rivaled that of even some of the most beloved goddesses of Olympus. We fell in love, but she was a mortal, and I an everlasting being... it seemed we were destined to fail from the start." I sigh, the pain still lingering despite the millennia of time passed.

"Despite our barrier, we aimed to live each moment like it could be our last. So, when Mother came to us, offering a way where we could be together, outside the limitations of mortal life, we thought our plight resolved."

"What was the offer?"

"Psyche would have to go through a set of godly trials to prove her devotion. If she were to pass each one, she would be granted immortality."

"Oh dear... she didn't die in the trials, did she?" Her hand flies over her mouth.

"No, no, nothing like that. She made it through one trial before she came to me with her reservations about becoming immortal. I suggested she take some time away from the trials, and I would find a way that I could become mortal. I would have done anything for her, even if that meant the eventual end of my existence."

"That sounds like true love." Her brows pinch together, and I know how familiar she is with that feeling.

"For me, it was." I sigh, glancing into the fountain waters. "Amidst the second trial, it was revealed that her heart was not true, for she loved another man—a mortal man."

She gasps, this time a hand flying over her heart.

"Instead of biding her time until I could find a way for us to be together, she ran off with the human. And to top it all off, she left all of this in a note she left by a lantern."

"Oh, Eros..." She pads over to me, and I stare at where she places a gentle hand on my arm, the contact feeling like a burst of fire. Looking into her eyes that catch the warm firelight, I see the understanding that lingers behind them. "I'm so sorry that she hurt you like that. You were willing to give up your immortality. You loved her."

"But she didn't love me the same. Alas, why I became a Scrooge when it came to love."

"A what?" She asks with raised brows. Oh right, I forgot she wouldn't know that yet. Silly me. "I believe you'd call me a spoilsport or a grouch." I over enunciate the words.

"You spoke in past tense." She almost whispers, taking a step back when she realizes her hand was still on my arm, and I immediately miss the feel of her skin.

"Hmm?" I ask, my thoughts having gotten lost on her.

"You said when it *came* to love. Are you starting to believe again?"

"Oh, well... seeing you put your heart out there despite your curse, seeing how you long for something so deep and emotional, it's making me think that real love does still exist."

"Thank you for sharing that with me. I know it

couldn't have been easy."

"Well, you've made life more bearable these past weeks." She looks down with a small smile, trying to hide her blush. "Thank you."

"For what?" Her soft brown eyes fall on me curiously.

"You've been helping me remember what love can be."

15

ALORA

As soon as Eros sends me home, a rushed knocking makes me whirl towards the door.

"Alora, open up already!" Gilda knocks slowly and rests her forehead against the glass. When I turn the knob, she backs up, relief washing over her face.

"Finally! I've only been knockin' for an eternity." She huffs sarcastically as she strides in past me.

"Sorry, Gilda. I must've been lost in thought." I smile.

"Oh, I bet you were..." She laughs, placing her

hands on her hips.

"Where in the blazes did you find that fine piece of a man?" She fans her face, feigning a swoon, and I laugh.

"We met in the forest. I was—on a walk." I point my finger in the air, emphasizing my thoughts.

"And what was this first meetin' like? All the details, nothin' left out!" She sits on the side of my bed, turning towards me in anticipation.

"Well, Eros—I mean Amo—" Before I can finish, the god pops up behind me in a puff of glittering magic, wings on full display. *Oh no.*

"Yes, love?" His melodic voice comes from behind us, and I shrink back.

"Buddin' daisies!" Gilda screams, falling off the bed in surprise, and Eros says what we are both thinking.

"F**k." **(Did you just bleep out f**k? I am warranted one use of the word to keep this PG-13 for movie adaptation's sake. Save it for a better use? This was a perfectly reasonable time for f**k.)**

"I—" I stand quickly, trying to explain, but I'm not really sure how to start.

"What the hell?" Gilda pops up from over the other

side of the bed, glancing wildly between Eros and me. “Who—what—"

“I didn’t mean to summon you.” I turn to Eros, an amused smile on his lips.

“I can see that.” He chuckles.

“Okay, Gilda; you know how I’ve always had rotten luck with men?” She stands hesitantly, peeling her eyes away from Eros slowly, like he’ll disappear if she’s not looking at him.

“Yes...” She says, drawing out the word.

“Well, I’m cursed. And I found these ancient ruins and summoned Cupid, who turned out to be Eros, to help me break it.” She looks at me dumbfounded, her lips parted as if to speak, but no words come out. When she turns her gaze towards Eros again, he smiles at her, wiggling his fingers in a wave.

“Oh, bleeding skies! I’d say you were mad if I didn’t just see this winged fellow pop up out of nowhere—a mighty handsome fellow though, if I do say.”

I let out a relieved laugh at Gilda’s last words.

“I knew I liked you.” Eros winks at Gilda, who flushes a bright pink. "I suppose I'll leave you two ladies to converse." before he disappears in a haze of rosy magic, he blows us a cheeky kiss, and I make sure he catches my eye roll before he's gone.

"What the ever-loving hell, Alora! You kept that masterpiece of a man from me?" Gilda playfully swats my arm.

"I wanted to tell you, but I wasn't sure what the rules were for working with Greek gods." I say, sitting back on the edge of my bed.

"So, he's helping ya find love is he? You were both mighty convincing at dinner." She says, sitting beside me, nudging me with her elbow in jest.

"It was just pretend, so I could avoid further attention from the horrid men the Winton's keep setting me up with."

"If a god looked at me the way Eros looked at ya, I'd melt on the spot." She swoons.

"He does his job well." I laugh, trying to hide my reddening cheeks as I remember the events of this evening.

"Mhmmm. I'm sure he was just doing his job."

"I actually have a date with a man I met at the museum." I say, changing the subject.

"Do ya now?" She waggles her eyebrows at me, making me giggle, but the lighthearted laughter fades to sorrow when the reality of it all sinks in.

"Is it foolish of me to think this will actually work? That someone could possibly fall in love with me?"

"Having hope for something you desire is never foolish." Gilda rubs a comforting hand up and down my arm.

"I—I just want to be cured." Sometimes, I think it'd be so much easier if I was like everyone else. To feel the way you're supposed to when it comes to love." I avert my gaze to my lap, where I fiddle with my fingers.

"My darling girl, the cure you need is not for something you are. You don't need to change to find love. You only need this blasted curse lifted that keeps it from finding you."

I know that she's right, but it often seems like I'm just floating through this limbo, alone and exiled from the rest of society because I haven't experienced what they have or feel what they feel.

"You always have the right thing to say. Thank you,

Gilda." I meet her gentle gaze with a smile. Hopefully, someday soon, I'll be able to believe that for myself.

16

Now that Gilda knows about my curse and Eros, I feel a bit lighter being able to share that with someone, especially someone like Gilda, who I trust and value so much. She's been asking questions non-stop ever since that evening, but it's almost therapeutic to be able to talk about it so openly, and I think it's made us even closer.

She insisted on coming over to help me ready for the ball this evening and get her fill on my potential suitor.

"Do you think this one could break your curse?" She asks as I powder my face.

"He seems kind, but it's too early to tell. Sometimes things go really well with a suitor... and then all of a sudden, it's like they realize they'll never love me."

"That's so unfair. Damn your ancestor." Gilda curses towards the sky.

"Most of them don't even seem to make it to that realization point. What runs them off apparently, is my lack of physical attraction towards them." Gilda's eyes catch mine in the mirror, a sadness behind them.

"Those blasted buffoons. Well, they're not worth your time anyway, and I'll pummel any right one of 'em that tries to insult you." She waves her fists in the air.

"Thanks, Gilda! You're the best!"

"So is Eros like your fairy godmother?" She asks, and I laugh, knowing he'd find it amusing also.

"I guess you could say that." Now that I think about it, he has been catering to my whims.

"Well, he is a sight to behold, that one. Got a nice tush on him too."

"Gilda!" I dramatically gasp. "Are you objectifying him?"

"I suppose I am. I mean, we once worshipped the gods right? I'm just reverin' his beauty, I am." She quips, and I shake my head at her antics. "Now, let's get you something to wear." She walks over to my closet, her mouth falling open in shock.

"These are stunnin'!"

"My woodland scraps?" I chuckle as I walk over, surprised when I see a whole row of beautiful gowns that were definitely not there before. *Eros!* I run my hand along the silky materials, my eyes getting caught on a lovely dark pink dress with a lace overskirt and short puffed sleeves threaded with beaded flowers.

"My, that is lovely. You're gonna make the man drool at the sight of you."

A knock at the door makes my heart flutter, Gilda rushing over to peek out.

"He's here! Oh, and he's handsome."

"Alright, how do I look? I smooth over my hair, half tied up with pearls, already feeling clammy from my nerves.

"You're dazzlin'!" She beams. Once I give my go-ahead, she opens the door. Avin looks incredibly dapper in his dark trousers, dark blue tailcoat, and elegant cravat, his coiled curls sculpted perfectly atop his head. He smiles almost nervously, and it makes me wonder if I actually have a chance with him.

"Hi." He gives a small wave.

"Hi." I give an awkward wave back, Gilda looking between the two of us.

"Well, aren't you two cute." She grins, placing a hand to her heart.

"Shall we?" He extends his arm out, my heart growing giddy as I link mine with his. My smile falters slightly as I remember where this kind of hope has led me before and rein myself in slightly.

Helping me into the carriage, he sits across from me as I fiddle with the lace of my gloves nervously.

"I have to admit—" He's jerked forward by the sudden start of the carriage, his left hand grasping the seat, his right accidentally grasping my knee. As soon as he realizes where his touch landed, he pulls back quickly, apologizing profusely.

"I'm terribly sorry! I didn't mean to—"

"It's quite alright. You were nearly lurched from your seat." I chuckle, assuring him that I'm not upset, and his horrified expression softens.

"I must say, I've been quite nervous for tonight."

"Really?" I ask, perhaps with a bit too much excitement. That's a good sign, right? *He's* nervous! Maybe I really do have a chance.

"Me too." I admit. "We can be nervous together, then." I smile shyly, his lips turning up into a grin.

When the carriage jolts to a halt in front of our destination, this time, Avin is prepared, holding onto the seat for dear life. Hopping out onto the graveled lot, he holds out his gloved hand for me to take.

Anticipation buzzes through me as we enter the grand ballroom, women in pastel gowns of lace and silk filling up the space, speckled with the dark accent of the men's attire. The glossy finish on the light-wood floor looks like a freshly frozen sheet of ice on a lake, and the cream walls are adorned with a gold filigree design, but it's the ceiling that has me in awe. A sky-blue color swirled with white and pink strokes to mimic clouds stretches across the slightly domed ceiling, shimmering gold paint outlining each one, the chandelier descending down like raindrops, a gentle glow emanating through the entire room.

I come down from my wonder when I feel Avin's arm stiffen in mine.

"Are you alright?" I ask as I turn to look at him, his lips in a thin line.

"Mmhm, yes." He says, perhaps a bit too quickly to be believable, but when he smiles down at me, I decide to not prod any further.

"May I get you a drink?"

"That would be lovely, but not champagne, please."

"I'll be right back with the drinks." He gives a slight bow before heading for the refreshments table. With my hands clasped before me, I glance around the room as people mingle. My heart nearly stops when my gaze lands on one couple.

The Wintons!

Oh, no! No, no no! They can't see me here with another man. They think I'm exclusively being courted by 'Amos.' Nervously glancing at where Avin is caught in a conversation, I sneak out onto one of the balconies.

"Eros! Emergen—" His tall, slender figure pops up in front of me before I even fully get the words out, and I jump in shock.

"I told you to stop doing that!" I lightly swat his arm, my heart thudding hard against my chest.

"I love how you scold me. No one has ever dared; it makes me feel special." He gives me that flirty look, and I roll my eyes.

"Eros, this is a serious situation. The Wintons are here!" I point a finger back towards the crowd, shrinking behind the drapes as to not be seen.

"Oh, that is a problem. They think I—well, Amos—is courting you."

"Exactly!"

"Not to worry, we will just give them a nice little

show to solidify our façade, then you'll be out of their mind as they enjoy the rest of the party."

"But I'm here with Avin. I don't want him to think I'm not serious about pursuing a courtship with him."

"I might regret this, but..." With a snap of his fingers, Dionysus appears beside him, his face lighting up when he sees me.

"ALORA!" He pulls me into a strong embrace, a chuckle spilling out of me at the god's excitement of seeing *me*.

"You're here on a mission, Dionysus, so behave." Eros points a stern finger at him.

"Yes, sir!" He says sarcastically with a salute, grinning wide when he sees he made me laugh.

"Your job is to distract Avin, Alora's date, as we have a quick dance to uphold our farce."

"Is there alcohol?"

"There's champagne." I interject, and Dionysus's face twists in revulsion.

"That horrid stuff? Good thing I always bring my own then, huh?" He winks as he pulls out a fancy bottle of wine out of thin air. "I got you covered!" He points at me before turning to walk into the ballroom, but Eros grabs him by the back of his toga, and Dionysus dramatically halts with an '*erg.*'

"Change first, you idiot."

"Oh, right." Snapping his fingers together, a dark purple outfit appears on his body, his crown no longer atop his head, then he saunters inside. Eros palms a hand to his face, regretting his call already.

Changing into his Amos attire, Eros extends out his arm to walk us back inside.

"Let's do this, shall we?"

17

EROS

Leading us to the dance floor, we stop at the center of the other couples as we wait for the music to begin.

"May I have this dance?" I bow slightly, extending my hand out to Alora as the first hum of strings fills the room.

"You may." She smiles, taking my hand.

“I didn’t know they’d be here. We have to make it look like we’re properly falling for each other.” She glances nervously past the other dancers to where Mr.

and Mrs. Winton stand, watching the gathering.

"Not a problem, love. I have quite the experience in the realm of passion." I wink playfully.

"Is that so? If I didn't know any better, I would think you might try and seduce me." She lets out a small laugh as we move to the music.

I guide her out of my arms, spinning her until her back is flat against my chest, her arms holding on to mine wrapped around her. Craning my neck down so my lips are at the shell of her ear, I whisper low enough for only her to hear.

"*If* I were trying to seduce you, I would tell you how breathtaking you are, or how this dress compliments every curve of your body—and it's pink. *My* color... was that on purpose?" When I pull back and spin her to face me, I can see the warmth rising to her skin, a grin spreading across my lips.

"Or maybe I would tell you how I admire your resolve in the face of struggle." She looks into my eyes as if trying to decipher if my words hold true. "I would tell you how soft your skin is and how good it feels beneath my fingers." I lead a light trail of my knuckles down the skin of her spine. She shutters under my touch as her breath gets caught in her throat, and I can't help but smile at the redness of her cheeks as she tries to avoid my gaze.

All of a sudden, the live musicians begin playing *"I Could Have Danced All Night,"* the couples around us breaking out into a choreographed dance that is not of this era.

Soon, my feet begin leading Alora in the elegant movements of those around us as the grand symphonic version of the song plays around us. **(I may be a god, but I don't make the rules for musical dance numbers.)**

We whirl around the room, light as feathers on our feet, each woman twirling in perfect sync with their partner as the song is covered by whatever celebrity they'll inevitably cast for the movie adaptation. *And still could have begged for more.* **(Oh, dear me...no, no, no.)** *I could have spread my wings*—involuntarily, my wings fan out in a big swoosh, guiding Alora and me backwards across the smooth stone floor as my wings catch a mystical wind. **(Of course, musical**

numbers suspend disbelief, so no one here bats an eye at the handsome winged man.)

This is all so absurd, but I can't help but get lost in the magic of the performance, Alora glowing as her hair sweeps around her, my heart thundering in my chest as she smiles widely at me.

She glides effortlessly through the air as I lift her by the waist, her skirts floating ethereally around her. As soon as her feet hit the floor, we break out into a tap dance during an instrumental, with, of course... a costume change. **(No... I do not know how to tap, but again, I don't make the rules. The magic of musical theater is beyond my control.)**

Now being the only couple on center floor, the rest of the world fades away as we glide together, hand in hand, along the curve of people. As the music slows, our feet leave the floor as we ascend towards the gaudy ceiling, nothing but her and me as we swirl around slowly in a haze of my magic.

Spinning her out once more, our eyes lock as I dip her during our descent. Once we reach the floor, my wings retract, the melody coming to an end as the rest of the room reenters my vision. As the last chord rings, I bring her back up slowly, her heart pounding like a hummingbird, our breaths mingling in the small space between us.

We stand there in the silence for a moment, still glued to each other's bodies as everyone dances around us, blissfully unaware of my heart threatening to burst. At this moment in time, it's just us, gazing into each other's eyes as if we seek the truth behind them.

Snapping out of my stupor, I step back with a bow.

"How's that for a show?" She blinks several times before answering.

"Erm..." she trails off, looking over to where the Winton's stand with warm smiles on their faces.

"I'd say it worked." She finishes, her tone holding a slight disappointment despite our success.

As we meld back into the crowd, I spot Avin making his way over, obviously trying to leave behind a persistent Dionysus. I subtly alert him to stop his pursuit with a tick of my head, and he disappears. **(No one can see us if we don't want them to, remember?**

Not like you all pay attention to your surroundings anyway.)

"Sorry about that. Some wine fanatic trapped me in conversation." He huffs a laugh, handing over a glass to Alora.

"Lord Oakton!" A man shouts from behind him.

"I'm sorry, would you excuse me for a moment?" He turns to address the man after Alora nods kindly. Taking a sip of her drink, her face immediately sours.

With a subtle wave of my hand, the liquid in her cup bubbles a bit less, the color lightening.

"Try it now." She looks at me quizzically before tasting it, her face now turning up in surprise.

"That's delicious!"

"White grape juice." I nod. "Have fun on your date, my love. I'll check in later." Before I'm about to transport, her laced-glove hand gently finds my arm.

"Thank you so much, Eros. For everything." Her brown eyes hold such sincerity, the glow from the chandelier bringing out those gold flecks, and I nearly get lost in them.

"You're most welcome, Alora." I hesitate a moment, staring at the place where she touched me, a burning sensation lingering behind. Hmm, what an odd thing.

18

EROS

As soon as I land back at my abode, I'm dumbstruck by a revelation from what I just experienced.

"You have feelings for Alora!" Dionysus shouts, barreling forward, and wrapping me in an embrace.

"I just got home." He pulls back, beaming at me.

"Sorry, sorry—that was quite the sight to see back at the ball. You know, the whole dance number and...costume change." He giggles at that last bit. "I think I'm rubbing off on you."

"Oh gods, you saw it all?" I swoop Muggsy up from the floor, petting his soft fur to calm my nerves. Since when have I ever been *nervous*?

"I can multitask, especially when it's something as entertaining as that. So, what are you going to do?"

"What do you mean?"

"You have to tell her how you feel."

"I'm doing no such thing!"

"Ha, you didn't deny it! It's true!" Dionysus claps his hands together with a wide grin.

"Listen, it's been a long night—"

"Say no more, I'll let you ruminate on your discovery, my friend!" Dionysus backs away, trying not to smile before disappearing.

With a heavy sigh, I find myself lost on what to do. I haven't felt this way about anyone since... Psyche. Perhaps I should talk to Mother. Calling one of my sparrows, I place a pink rose petal in its talons.

"Please deliver this to Aphrodite and notify her that I'll be arriving soon." The little bird gives a tiny nod before taking flight. I can't believe this... maybe I've mistaken my feelings for lo—the L word. My gods, I can't even say it. When my sparrow returns, I take a swig of whiskey before heading over to Mothers.

Appearing in her stunning seaside home, I fiddle with my fingers, hoping the alcohol does its job soon enough.

"My dear, how are you?" Arms open wide, Mother walks over, her hair swishing back and forth. "How are things going with the woman—Alora, was it?"

"Right, yes—Alora. It's going well, *too well.*" I say under my breath, and if Mother hears, she gratefully pretends she hasn't.

"Eros, you seem troubled. Sit; let us talk." She gestures over to the seashell chairs, and I sit with a heavy sigh.

"I—something has happened, and I don't quite know what to do about it." I glance nervously up at Mother's shimmering eyes, a small smile gracing her face.

"You're in love." She says it as a statement rather than a question.

"How did you know?" Those little wings flutter in my heart when I don't deny it. I *am* in love.

"It's all over your face, my boy. And I have, from time to time, been overseeing your progress with Alora. I see the way you look at her—the effect she has on you."

"But I cannot feel this way about her. She is a mortal, and she is cursed." I sigh heavily.

"Psyche was a mortal." She says, and I nearly glare at her for mentioning that woman but decide I quite like living.

"Yes, and we see how well that turned out." I huff. "Besides, Psyche was not cursed. Alora is forced to suffer from unrequited love. No one is to love her until the curse can be broken."

"We both know my curses can get quite intense, but I am not unreasonable. There is always a way around a curse, though it may not be easy." She gives me that grin that she always does when she knows something I don't.

"How do you mean?" I ask hesitantly.

"Alora's mother... she experienced the same curse and wanted nothing more than for her daughter to not have to deal with her same plight. Her love for

Alora transcended beyond the curse and opened a loophole."

"What sort of loophole?"

"Well, you know when she summoned me, but I sent you in my stead because I was buried in prayers?"

"Yes..." I furrow my brows at her, my voice rising in pitch as I await her next words.

"That wasn't quite the truth. I indeed could have answered Alora, but I left it to you..." She trails off, leaving me to process the rest.

"Great Olymp—I'M THE LOOPHOLE?" I stand abruptly, taken aback by this new information. "Mother, how could you? Are my feelings for her even true?" I feel a slight panic as I say the words aloud. She stands hurriedly, placing a gentle hand on my arm to reassure me.

"Eros, your feelings are all your own. It was not a sure outcome, but it was an *opportunity* for Alora's curse to be broken. There was no guarantee you would fall in love with her; I just merely presented the chance—much like your arrows do." She smiles softly at me.

“My gods, you are one sneaky goddess, Mother.” I exhale, placing my hands on my hips as I try to get a handle on myself. “So, is her curse broken then? If—if another man falls for her...” I run a hadn't through my hair, not able to remember the last time *I* felt anxious.

“It is not broken yet. Your confession to her must be uttered aloud.”

“I—what if she doesn’t feel the same? I don’t know if I can go through this again.”

“Is it a chance you’re willing to take to find out if your feelings are reciprocated?" Her words land heavily on my heart as I pace back and forth, trying to wrap my head around this all. What mother says next stops me in my tracks. "If you never confess your love, her curse will continue.”

19

ALORA

With Eros gone, I feel like he took all the warmth with him. Big social gatherings have never been my forte, and with Avin stuck in conversation, I stand awkwardly in my spot, sipping on my sparkling juice as I watch people mingle.

“Alora," Avin says as he moves through bodies towards me. "I apologize for that. I keep getting trapped in conversation with everyone this evening." He chuckles under his breath.

“That’s alright." I smile. "You’re very popular.”

"Would you like to take a walk through the gardens? Perhaps we can finally talk without interruption." He asks, his eyes quickly glancing to the French doors leading outside.

"That sounds lovely." Placing down my drink, I take his arm. We walk out into the maze of tall shrubbery. It's not as impressive as Eros's Garden, but still pretty. We walk together on the plush grass in silence for a bit, the stars sparkling in the sky, and I wonder why there's this ache in my chest.

"So, Alora. What's something you enjoy?" Avin breaks the silence.

"I adore nature and all its lovely creatures. Sometimes I like to lie in a nice patch of grass beneath a tree and read a good book."

"That sounds like a lovely time." He grins.

"What do you enjoy?"

"I actually love to paint." His eyes light up when he says it, and I can sense the passion he has for art.

"You're an artist?" I ask, a bit surprised, but his awe at the work in the museum was evident.

"Ha, not quite. But someday, I hope to have one

of my works hanging in a gallery or even better, on someone's wall." He looks off into the distance with a sparkle in his eye, imagining the scene.

"I bet one day, many will want to own an *Avin Oakton Original.*" I emphasize with a hand, smiling at his bashful grin.

We pass a few people giggling around a fountain before we come to a section that veers off in two directions.

"Which path shall we take?" He asks, his gaze bouncing between the two paths.

"Hmm." I tap a finger to my chin. "I'm feeling left."

"Really? I was going to say right. Do you think they converge?" He leans down to whisper.

"Well, I guess there's only one way to find out." I say playfully and he quirks up a brow at the challenge.

"See you on the other side." He says, then we run off onto our own paths, and I can't help the laughter that spills out of me. The shrubs are much thicker than I realized, his footsteps dwindling the further in we get, and I'm wondering if our long paths actually converge when I have to slow to a walk.

When I finally see a curve in the path ahead, I smile excitedly, curious if Avin's already made it. Slowing down when I reach the corner, I can hear a voice—wait, no—*voices*. Peeking around the edge, my smile fades when I see Avin talking to a woman in a lilac-colored dress.

"It wasn't my choice, Avin." The woman shakes her head, tears brimming in her eyes.

"I thought I could get over you, but then I saw you tonight, and I—" He starts, but she stops him short, and my stomach sinks at his words. That's why he's been so elusive. She was near every single conversation he had. What a fool I was.

"I wish it could be different. I still love you, but my family has already made the arrangements." She says not able to look him in the eyes.

"Run away with me, then." Avin takes her hands in his, hopeful.

I have to cover my mouth to keep in my gasp, but the movement catches the woman's eyes as she glances my way, Avin following her gaze. I quickly pull back behind the shrubbery, but I know I've been seen. I take a deep breath as the soft pad of footsteps grows near.

"Alora?" Avin's voice is soft as he says my name. "I'm sorry you heard that."

I slowly round the corner to face him, worry on his brow

"I'm not." He looks confused for a moment. "If your heart belongs to someone else, I'd rather know now than try to make this work only to end up heartbroken." I keep my mask of neutrality up, but what he doesn't know is that in that moment, my heart cracked a little at the hope I'd allowed myself to feel this time, betraying me.

"I never intended for the evening to go like this. I didn't expect to even see her here. I'm so sorry, Alora. You're truly so kind..."

As soon as he goes into telling me how great I am or whatnot, I sigh, not having it in me to hear what I've always heard, so I place up a hand to stop him.

"It's alright, Avin. If you're able to find the kind of love that transcends, then hold onto it. I truly hope it works out for you both." He looks a bit taken aback by my comment, but I mean it. Nobody deserves to be in a loveless relationship. With that, I leave him. Getting lost in the tall shrubbery, the tears flow freely, and the world feels like it's closing in on me now.

"Er—Eros!" My voice cracks slightly as I call his name, his comforting presence appearing right when I call him.

"How goes—" He immediately falters when he takes me in, his face turning down in concern. "Alora, love. What happened?" He gently cups my face, bending down to catch my gaze.

"Can you please get me out of here?" My question comes out as more of a plea, desperate to get away from all of this.

"Yes, yes. Are you ready?" He asks, and I nod quickly. In the blink of an eye, we're back at his place on Olympus. Collapsing onto the closest chair, I place my face in my hands, defeated. Muggsy hops up by my feet, chittering softly.

"What did he do? Do you need me to smite him?" Eros asks, trying to perk me up. Usually it would, but this was my last chance. After so many failed attempts, even with the god of love... my curse will never end.

"I should've known better. I can't believe I thought this time would be any different than the others." I look up from my palms, surely looking like a raccoon with all the tears.

"This isn't the end, Alora. There's—" He starts, but I stand in frustration, not even concerned that I'm cutting off a god.

"But he can't love me; no one has, no one can. It will never be." I huff a breathy laugh. "How foolish I was to think my curse could be broken, to hold out hope for such a lost cause." I place my hand to my forehead, tears burning my eyes as I look out into the endless night sky, swirling with purples and blues. There's a moment of silence before Eros steps closer.

"Alora, my love..." I turn to face him as he ruffles a hand through his hair, glancing down to the floor. For the first time, he almost looks—*nervous*."

"It is true that I failed to make a man fall in love with you." His eyes slowly flick up to find mine, a desperate plea behind them. Is he wanting my forgiveness, worried it's him I'm upset with? "But I managed to break the curse."

Taken aback, I shake my head with furrowed brows, not quite understanding.

"I'm sorry, what do you mean? A man didn't fall in love with me."

"Yes... but a *god* did." The words fall from his tongue like a prayer answered, the breath lost in my lungs as a gentle breeze blows against me, and I feel a warm sensation settling in my heart.

I close my eyes as it washes over me, my nose stinging as a tear falls from my eyes. I hear his footsteps pad towards me, his closeness sending a blush to my cheeks. My breath stutters as his gentle hand cups my face, wiping away the stray tear with his thumb, and I can't help but lean slightly into his palm.

When I open my eyes, there's a vulnerability in his, and now I understand his desperate plea.

"Alora Meadows, you have completely shaken my entire world. I never thought I'd feel the way I do with you, but you've changed the way in which I perceive love." His hand brushes ever so lightly from my cheek, across my collarbone, and down my arm until he finds my hand.

"I tell you now, as a god who has been worshipped for over a millennium, I've been on my knees for no one." I inhale sharply as his knees meet the glossy floor below us. When he looks up at me, his eyes are pooling with reverence. "But for you, I would live the rest of my days on my knees. I love you, Alora, so madly that I'd carve your name into the earth so that everyone knows I'm yours—if you'll have me."

I'm so overwhelmed by his confession that if he wasn't holding my hand, I feel as though I'd float away.

"Get up and kiss me." I say breathlessly. He smirks, wasting no time in crashing his lips to mine, and suddenly all the years spent feeling like I wasn't enough become a distant memory. When we pull away for air, he rests his forehead against mine as we both smile.

"Fuck, you taste as delicious as I thought you would." **(You're right, Ms. Everwood; that was a better use of the word.)**

I blush furiously, Eros eyeing where my skin flushes down my neck, his pupils blowing wide as his gaze travels further.

"So, you'll bow before me *and* answer my commands." I wrap my arms around his neck, our noses brushing.

"I'm at your mercy, my love. I'll do whatever you ask of me." His hands smooth down my waist to rest on my hips, and my knees nearly turn to jelly. I melt into him as he kisses me again, not wanting to part despite my lungs begging for air. "I'm not going anywhere, my love." He whispers against my lips.

"I'm afraid this is all just a dream, and I don't want you to disappear." I look into his soft blue eyes to ground me in this moment.

"It's all very real... and guess who we have to thank for it all?"

"Who?" I ask, breathlessly.

"My mother."

"Aphrodite herself?" I say, completely shocked by this reveal.

"Mhmm. Apparently, she was playing Cupid all along. Maybe I should be concerned about losing my job."

"I doubt that, now that you believe in love and

all." I grin, wrapping my arms around his neck, pressing my lips to his again.

"And if it weren't for you, my heart would still be as cold as the marble statue of me." He kisses the tip of my nose.

"I love you, Eros." I whisper in the small space between us, and his eyes sparkle as they flick up to mine.

"I love you, Alora. I knew from the moment you almost fell into my statue's arms that eventually you'd fall into mine." His words feel like a gentle caress, soothing my rapidly beating heart.

A loud clapping startles us from our kiss, and we turn to see Dionysus watching us as he continues to cheerfully clap.

"I've been waiting for you two to kiss; this is spectacular! The curse is broken!" He shouts before disappearing. Well, at least he can read a room.

"How do you feel, my love? Any different now that the curse is broken?" I brush a strand of hair behind her ear, placing a gentle kiss on the tip of her nose.

"Well, I can say truthfully that I'm definitely no longer lovelorn." Then she kisses me so passionately,

I almost forget I'm the ancient deity. And like I said, I plan to worship her as though she is one, kissing her back with just as much ferocity.

(A little privacy, please...shoo, shoo.)

Epilogue

EROS

"No longer being scorned by love, I find my job much more enjoyable, but I attribute most of that to the stunning new partner I have—"

"ME!" Dionysus shouts loudly as he wraps an arm around me, Alora chuckling at my annoyance.

"Dionysus, I'm trying to tell the readers how this ends." I shake my head at him.

"Oh, I can tell them!" Dionysus shoves his way between me and Alora. "Lots of smooching, tons of flirty looks across the room, their hands are all over each other—it's disgusting really." Alora lets out a hearty laugh as I push Dionysus out of the way as he continues to spout off nonsense.

"Anywho... as you know, Dionysus was very ecstatic

when he heard the news of me and Alora, but I think he was even more excited to have made a new eternal friend. Oh right, Alora was granted immortality. It was a whole thing; we had a ceremony, an afterparty, all that jazz."

"It was me who ended up in a diaper this time." Dionysus shouts with a big smile pasted on his face.

"That's not something to be proud of. I digress. We had long talks about how we would live out our lives and if Alora even wanted immortality. I offered to live out our lives as humans, however shriveled and pruney we may become. Here, why don't I just show you... come to the fountain.

Shortly after the confession:

"Eros?" Her voice comes out soft from where she rests her head on my shoulder.

"Yes, my love?"

"Forever is a long time—something I can't truly begin to fathom." I gently trace a pattern up and down her back.

"I know it's a long time to live—"

"That's not it." She plays with the fabric of my sash,

a telltale sign that she's nervous.

"What's wrong, my love?"

"Well, you know in the past, my relationships were never... physical. And I just don't feel the same way that most people do when it comes to that kind of intimacy."

Ahh, I see where her thoughts worry her.

"My love..." I sit up slightly, and she looks up at me, a vulnerableness in those brown eyes that I love so much. "You don't owe me anything just because we're together."

"But, forever..." I sit up fully now, gently bringing her chin to look at me.

"Whether our relationship remains intellectual and emotional or somewhere along the way develops physically, it doesn't matter to me as long as it's you that I'm with." Just as I finish my words, I see the walls breaking down that she's held up for so long, finally feeling free to be herself entirely, without judgment.

"I do quite like the kissing bit." She looks up at me through her lashes, biting her bottom lip—and there goes that fluttering of wings in my chest.

"I like that part, too."

"Okay, okay—you don't need to see the rest of that,

you little beasts."

"Hey, I was watching that." Dionysus frowns as the memory ripples away.

"Of course you were, you voyeur." I shake my head at him.

"Anyway, as you can see—" (SNAP, SNAP) you, reader... over here. I'm talking to you now.

"It was very sweet, very intimate, so suck it all up while you can because that's all you're going to—"

Don't go breaking my heart. Elton John's voice reverberates through the air.

"Oh, gods; what's happening?"

I couldn't if I tried.

"As you can see, Alora and Eros healed something in each other."

"Who the hell is that?" I look up towards the voice coming from nowhere and everywhere all at once as the song continues to play.

"Shut up, Eros. It's the narrator—he's narrating."

Dionysus shushes me. My lips part, about to protest, but Alora bounds over.

"Just let it happen." She kisses me on the cheek before grabbing me by the hand and leading me through the garden.

"**A god, down on love, and a woman cursed, the pair taught each other a new meaning of the word as they slowly fell for each other.**"

Dionysus spins around with Muggsy in his arms as if in slow motion before the perspective shifts back to me and Alora, running through a tunnel of flowers.

"Alora learned that she doesn't have to earn love to be worthy of it, and Eros learned to open his heart again to more than just a hare and a fern."

This is ridiculous; I'm the one who's supposed to be telling the story. Just then, Alora stops and turns to me.

"You're the one who gets to live it." She says with a devious smile on her lips before she grabs me by the front of my sash, pulling me behind the shrubs, and crashing her lips to mine.

I can get behind that idea.

"And they both lived happily ever after."

THE END

Cupid (Eros)..................Played by *not* a chubby cherub

Alora..................................Played by a disney princess

Muggsy................................Played by the cutest hare

Radford...............................Played by the cutest fern

Dionysus............................Played by the handsomest god

Aphrodite.....................Played by the fairest of them all

Gilda...Played by Gilda

Mrs. Winton..........................Played by Mrs. Winton

Mr. Winton..............................Played by Mr. Winton

Bernath Tinswell...............Played by insecure manchild

Avin Oakton.........................Played by Avin *Joke*ton

Cecil...Played by rat-faced man

Peter Wylington.......................Played by an asshole

Acknowledgements

This story is one I started just for fun, but it also holds a very special place in my heart, having put some of my own thoughts and struggles into Alora. While I wanted to make people laugh, I also wanted to showcase moments of reality when it comes to love, or lack thereof. For everyone who chose this story to read, thank you for supporting me. And for anyone who identified with Alora, you are not alone.

As with any story, I wouldn't be where I am without the support and encouragement from some amazing people.

To each one of you who signed up for ARCs, thank you so much for being interested in my work and for taking the time to read this story. The joy I got when the names popped up gave me even more excitement for this project to finally be out in the world. When I received messages and reviews from people who really felt the themes of Lovelorn and found themselves reflected in my characters in any way, it is truly a writer's dream and exactly why I love writing stories that are grounded in parts of reality but with a backdrop of a fantastical world.

Lauren Baker, my wonderful editor and author friend, you are one of the best cheerleaders around! If it weren't for your constant support—in the highs and the lows—I wouldn't be where I'm at with the millions of stories I have. Thank you for being down for all of my creative projects, pushing me to continue with each one, and for believing in me, as well as this story.

C.A Farran, you are always such an inspiration with your creativity and your stunning works. You never fail to listen to my podcast long audios where I go on and on about life, my current obsessions, and my story ideas. You always help fuel me forward, encouraging me every step of the way, even when you're working on your own projects. Thank you so much for being in my corner and matching my excitement for writing projects!

Nadine, thank you so much for always boosting me up and listening to my ideas and fangirling over them as much as me. You are always there to lend an ear, whether it be to talk about life, stories, or current obsessions (A.K.A, Aldi finds of the week.) I appreciate your friendship so much and am honored to have you in my corner.

Brandi Gann, you have always been such an amazing friend and support system, lifting me up when I get down on myself. I love how you caught all the 90s & early 2000s rom-com references. Your excitement for this project made me even more excited, and I appreciate you being there for all of my endeavors!

Emmi Finkenfügel, you are an absolute delight! I can't tell you enough how incredible you are as a person, an artist, and a friend. You are such a constant support, always carving out time to read my stories despite the craziness of life. When I got your feedback, I was so over the moon at how much you enjoyed it. You are such an inspiration to my creativity, and I'm so grateful to know you!

ABOUT THE AUTHOR

ALYSHA EVERWOOD grew up obsessed with Greek mythology and rom-coms. Always wanting to write a book inspired by her love for the myths, she waited for the right story inspiration to strike. Taking a break from writing her fantasy series--and the countless random ideas--the story came after she decided Lovelorn would be a great title for a book. Missing the feeling of what romantic comedies of the early 2000s brought to the table, she let her imagination and humor run wild, this project allowing her creativity to flow freely. Creating this story, she hoped it would connect with people who have ever felt similar to the themes explored in this novella.

www.ingramcontent.com/pod-product-compliance
Lightning Source LLC
LaVergne TN
LVHW090516110826
845146LV00003B/874

* 9 7 9 8 9 9 9 5 0 6 4 2 9 *